The door swung silently inward, and Bolan eased himself through

Carved wooden balusters railed in the gallery, which was in deep shadow. The room below was lit by three green-shaded lamps that hung poolroom-style over the vast table.

Bolan lowered himself to the floor and peered down between two balusters.

A big ornate chair at the head of the table was empty. Sanguinetti, the owner of the property—Bolan recognized him from newspaper photos—was installed at the foot. The other ten men were ranged five on either side. They were talking among themselves.

Bolan could make out no individual words, could hear no names. He did not need to. The Executioner realized that he was looking at ten of the most powerful men in the world.

And the most evil.

MACK BOLAN
The Executioner

DON PENDLETON's EXECUTIONER

MACK BOLAN

Sunscream

A GOLD EAGLE BOOK FROM

WORLDWIDE

TORONTO · NEW YORK · LONDON · PARIS
AMSTERDAM · STOCKHOLM · HAMBURG
ATHENS · MILAN · TOKYO · SYDNEY

First edition January 1986

ISBN 0-373-61085-8

Special thanks and acknowledgment to
Peter Leslie for his contributions to this work.

Printed in Canada

In memory of U.S. Navy Petty Officer Robert Stethem,
who was shot by Shiite hijackers
aboard TWA Flight 847 in Beirut, June 1985.

THE
MACK BOLAN
LEGEND

Nothing less than a war could have fashioned the destiny of the man called Mack Bolan. Bolan earned the Executioner title in the jungle hellgrounds of Vietnam, for his skills as a crack sniper in pursuit of the enemy.

But this supreme soldier also wore another name—Sergeant Mercy. He was so tagged because of the compassion he showed to wounded comrades-in-arms and Vietnamese civilians.

Mack Bolan's second tour of duty ended prematurely when he was given emergency leave to return home and bury his family. Bolan made his peace at his parents' and sister's gravesite. Then he declared war on the evil force that had snatched his loved ones. The Mafia.

In a fiery one-man assault, he confronted the Mob head-on, carrying a cleansing flame to the urban menace. And when the battle smoke cleared, a solitary figure walked away alive.

He continued his lone-wolf struggle, and soon a hope of victory began to appear. But Mack Bolan had broken society's every rule. That same society started gunning for this elusive warrior—to no avail.

So Bolan was offered amnesty to work within the system against international terrorism. This time, as an official employee of Uncle Sam, Bolan wore yet another handle: Colonel John Phoenix. With government sanction now, and a command center at Stony Man Farm in Virginia's Blue Ridge Mountains, he and his new allies—Able Team and Phoenix Force—waged relentless war on a new adversary: the KGB and all it stood for.

Until the inevitable occurred. Bolan's one true love, the brilliant and beautiful April Rose, died at the hands of the Soviet terror machine.

Embittered and utterly saddened by this feral deed, Bolan broke the shackles of Establishment authority.

Now the big justice fighter is once more free to haunt the treacherous alleys of the shadow world.

PROLOGUE

The water-skier's curving white wake mirrored a vapor trail in the azure sky above the Riviera. The bronzed man on a single ski swept into a final slalom before the speedboat towing him slowed down between the line of buoys leading to the jetty. The skier leaned back against the pull of the rope and the roar of the engine faded to a hum three markers out from the jetty. Two...one...

Suddenly an explosion lifted the surface of the sea.

When the tower of white water collapsed into the ocean, the speedboat, the two young men crewing it and the skier had all vanished.

There was pandemonium among sunbathers lying on the hot sand. A crowd had gathered along the railing of the palm-fringed promenade, excited voices rising above the chaos on the beach.

Farther along the promenade a man in a white sharkskin suit sat alone in a parked Mercedes. He slid a small detonating device into the glove compartment, then started the car. As he pulled out into traffic and headed for Cannes, he was smiling.

ONE HOUR LATER, a red and silver executive Jet began its descent toward the auxiliary runway on the seaward side of Nice International Airport. Circling over the blue crescent of the Baie des Anges, the pilot saw what seemed to be some kind of disturbance on one of the beaches. He could make out the red cross on an ambulance roof, and flashing amber roof lights of patrol cars. Traffic on the promenade was jammed as far as the Airport entrance.

The pilot dismissed it and concentrated on his descent. He turned to the expensively dressed man behind him. "Fasten your seatbelt, Mr. Ralfini. We're ready to touch down."

The owner of the jet nodded and snapped the belt's safety clasp together. "Make it a smooth one, Joe," he said.

The controller's voice in the pilot's earphones crackled last minute approach instructions. The pilot checked out the battery of lights on the instrument panel. Satisfied, he banked the aircraft and pointed the nose down. The long streak of runway rushed toward them.

The duty officer behind the green glass windows of the control tower watched the small jet come in. The sun was low and on the macadam surface of the runway, the aircraft's shadow lagged behind the speeding jet.

"Oh, no!" the officer shouted. "He's flying her into the ground...the landing gear isn't even down!" He grabbed the microphone from its cradle on the counter in front of him.

Too late. The racing shadow and the plane above drew closer. There was a puff of smoke as the two leaped together, then a livid flash momentarily dimmed the waning sunlight.

The shattering thump of the impact reached to the control tower, and the officer and his Number Two were on their feet, yelling into intercom mikes for fire trucks and the ambulance. By the time the salvage crews got to the field, the smoldering bodies of the pilot and his passenger were scarcely distinguishable from the charred wreckage around them.

FIVE THOUSAND MILES away on a hotel balcony overlooking Montego Bay in Jamaica, Alvaro Scotto buttered the two halves of a breakfast roll and spread them thickly with mango jam.

"Better than Marseilles, huh?" he said, addressing the attractive redhead on the far side of the table.

She looked out over the shimmering sweep of blue water. Half a dozen brightly colored fishing boats, back from the early trawl, were rounding the densely wooded point. "At least it smells better," she replied.

Scotto grinned. He stuffed the remainder of the roll into his mouth and then drained his coffee. He belched loudly and licked his fingers. "That's what I like about you, babe—you're so romantic," he said sarcastically.

The redhead tried to conceal her dislike of the man as she returned her gaze back to him. He was a squat, balding man, with black hair curling on his arms and along the backs of his fingers. The silk robe that he wore had parted over the pale paunch bulging above his thighs. "Who could be anything else, Al, with you around?" she said.

The boats were nearing the shore. Beyond a trio of early windsurfers, light flashed suddenly as the sun reflected off some polished surface.

Scotto picked up a glass of orange juice.

Splinters of crystal erupted from his fingers and fountained across the white clothed table. The girl started to her feet as the juice soaked the front of her green kimono. "You clumsy ape!" she yelled, pulling at the damp material.

Scotto was staring at the blood leaking from a hole in the palm of his hand.

The second slug took away the top of his head and catapulted him against the French windows leading to the room. The girl opened her mouth to scream.

The third bullet smashed through her front teeth and punched a fist-sized exit in the back of her skull. She fell forward across the table, her gory hair drenched in lukewarm coffee.

THREE HOURS LATER, on a long stretch of railway track in the center of France, a high-speed train was hitting something over 170 mph when three men stopped at the door of Compartment 9.

The tallest of the trio tapped on the maplewood panel. A voice from inside said something indistinguishable.

"Tickets, please," the tall guy called.

The door opened a crack. The three men shouldered it wide and crowded into the compartment. The bed was made up, the blinds pulled down. The occupant of the sleeper was a spare, gray-haired man of about sixty.

"What the hell...? Smiler! Wh—what do you guys want with me?" he blustered.

"I think you know, Frankie," Smiler said. "The capo don't go too strong on guys who welsh on a deal."

One of the men was carrying a briefcase. He opened it and took out a length of solid steel about eighteen inches long.

Frankie's face had blanched. Sweat dewed his forehead. "Look, you guys...*please*..." Swivelling on his heel, he made a desperate leap for the alarm cord above the window.

Smiler hit him expertly in the belly. He folded forward, retching. The man with the steel bar raised it high and smashed it savagely across Frankie's scalp.

Frankie went down. Blood gushed from his mouth, nose and ears, but Smiler was ready with a towel he had snatched from the rail beside the bunk.

"Dump him," Smiler ordered his two companions.

The two killers snapped open the blind and rolled down the wide window. Lights streaked past as the high-speed express rocketed over a crossing and roared through a deserted station. Once it was dark again they pushed Frankie's body through the gap and let it drop.

The man with the length of steel wiped it on the blood-stained towel and stowed both in his briefcase. Smiler closed the window and pulled down the blind.

Frankie's body, still traveling at more than 100 mph, hit the cinders, bounced high into the air and finally came to rest, hanging like some obscene fruit from a sapling halfway down the embankment.

His dead eyes stared sightlessly at the red lantern on the last car as the train vanished into the night.

1

"Coincidence?" Mack Bolan said. "Uh—uh. There is a link between those killings."

"Naturally, there is a link, *monsieur*," the Swiss Interpol chief agreed. "All four of them—"

"Were *mafiosi*? Sure. But there is something more. I can't see any connection between the four guys or the territories they worked, but those hits were put out by the same source. *Why were they killed within a few hours of one another*?"

"We were hoping, Monsieur Bolan, that maybe *you* could enlighten *us*," the superintendent from the French Counterintelligence Service put in. "You have a reputation as the most successful anti-Mafia fighter ever. That is why we asked you to come to this meeting."

"I thought I was on the blacklist," Bolan said.

The superintendent coughed. "The dossier has been...mislaid," he said. The warrior raised his hand to save further explanation. He had no fight with these men. They saw fit to call him in on this problem and that was all he cared about right now.

The three of them were sitting around a mahogany table in a private room on the fourth floor of a Geneva Hotel. Outside, squalls of rain blew across the lake and obscured the mountains to the east.

Bolan looked from one to the other of the two law-enforcement officers. "Four unrelated mobsters. We have to figure out what they'd been planning, separately or together, that was such dynamite."

The Frenchman, whose name was Chamson favored Bolan with a wintry smile. "It must have been a big deal." He turned to the Interpol chief. "Could we have another rundown on those killings, Telder?"

Colonel Telder picked up a document case, opened the case and took out a folder. From this he removed a single sheet of typescript and began to read aloud.

"Nice, France, early afternoon on the eleventh. Jean-Miguel Balestre—thirty one years old, tough, good looking—blown to pieces by a floating mine while water-skiing. Detonation of the explosive is thought to have been by remote control. Probably a radio beam. Balestre was Corsican, a fast-rising Cosa Nostra boss on the island.

"Same town, same day, a couple of hours later. Jan Ralfini, a district chief working for the Camorra in Naples, killed when his private jet crash-lands at the airport. Preliminary investigations suggest that landing gear, altimeter and warning lights had all been sabotaged.

"Half a world away in Montego Bay, Jamaica, morning of the eleventh. Alvaro Scotto and his mistress shot to death by a rifleman in a fishing boat. Scotto was one of several gang bosses who had agreed to a carve-up of the Marseilles territory.

"Three hours later, in central France, Frankie Secondini, a low-ranking *mafioso* from Paris, apparently falls from a train on his way to Marseilles." The colonel slipped the sheet of paper back into his case, then looked inquiringly at Bolan.

The Executioner watched the window rattling in its frame as wind scattered raindrops against the glass.

"Looks like typical Syndicate hits," Bolan said. "The method in each case was different, but they have one thing in common: ruthless efficiency." He turned to Chamson. "I believe you ran the four names through the Central Register computer in Paris. Come up with anything?"

"Nothing that looks like paydirt," the Frenchman said. "All of them were small-time bosses and all were into prostitution, protection rackets of one kind or another, and each had gambling connections."

"Drugs?"

"Only two—Ralfini and Balestre—are on the narcotics bureau files, and they didn't work the same circuits. Scotto smuggled arms; the others didn't."

Bolan hoisted his muscled, six-three frame from the chair and walked to the window. The killings intrigued him. Through countless bloody campaigns, he had broken the Mafia stranglehold on society in his own country, flushed away a good part of the slime-bucket corruption that threatened to pollute America and made the world safer for innocent civilizers. More recently he had fought international terrorism, in particular the hydra-headed conspiracy masterminded by Soviet Russia's infamous KGB. And it was because of a KGB plot, framing him for the murder of a European labor leader, that he was now an outlaw himself.

Lately, Bolan felt he had fought a successful containment action against the U.S. Mafia. Still, he considered it a minor victory, because he had no idea where the grim specter of the Mob would rise again! Well, now he knew.

"Any lead among the victims' effects?" Bolan asked.

"One," Chamson replied, taking a folded computer printout from an inside pocket. He smoothed it out on the table, before he spoke again. "Scotto was due to fly to Paris the day he was killed. He also had an onward book-ing to Marseilles. Secondini was headed for the same city. Ralfini was landing at Nice, but his pilot had already filed a second flight plan for later that evening. His destination was the Marseilles airport.''

"And Balestre?"

"He was due to check out of his hotel that evening, too. I think he and Ralfini would have flown to Marseilles together. Why else would the plane have landed at Nice?"

Bolan nodded slowly. "So the four of them had a meet fixed in Marseilles. And someone didn't want them to make it."

"That's the way we read it," Chamson said. "But why?"

Bolan was thoughtful. "I'm all for *mafiosi* liquidating one another. But in this case, I am curious. I think those four guys were aiming to horn in on something, but somehow it doesn't seem to stack up in this case. The details are vague at this point."

"It may not be as difficult as you think," Chamson said. "There was a fifth death, you see, that you don't know about."

"A fifth?" There was renewed interest in Bolan's voice.

"Not a murder this time. A fatal road accident. The victim was a hit man from Hamburg. He was headed for Marseilles to work for one of the gang bosses there. Not Scotto. But the four guys we're concerned with aren't the only ones to get on the wrong side of the mobsters."

"Go on," Bolan said.

"None of the Riviera hoods have met this gorilla. They've only seen photos. Nobody knows about the car smash: we kept the news under wraps."

Bolan said nothing.

"There's a distinct resemblance," Telder said. "With the minimum of disguise, you could pass for the German—you could get away with his ID." He paused for effect, then added, "We think it might be a good idea if you went to Marseilles in his place."

"Right," Bolan said, wryly understanding that while these people needed his expertise, he would still be regarded as an outlaw.

Chamson said, "We understand from certain rumors that have been filtering in for some time that something big is brewing in the Riviera underworld. But we have no idea what. It may not be connected with the four killings, but we thought that here was a perfect opportunity to find out from the inside. What do you say, *monsieur*?"

"I say it's a start," Bolan replied.

And that's all it was, nothing more, the big guy knew.

"But will you use it? Your feelings about the predators in our society are, as I said, no secret. We thought perhaps you would welcome the chance of striking another blow. We would stand by to give you any help we could." In his turn, Chamson paused. "Monsieur Bolan, *will* you help?"

"This Hamburg hit man—where did he die?" was all Bolan said.

2

It was night and the cold mistral wind was rushing down the Rhone Valley when Bolan pulled the BMW sedan off the expressway and drove through a deserted rest area to the gas station. No cars stood by the rows of brightly lit pumps, and as he coasted to a halt an attendant came out of the pay booth. "Fill her up?"

Bolan nodded, glancing beyond the booth to the refreshment bar as the man stooped to unscrew the gas tank's cap.

It was then that Bolan saw the boots, toes pointing skyward, protruding from behind the candy counter at the rear of the small shop.

And that the nozzle in the attendant's hand was attached not to a hose but to an 8-round magazine.

Bolan hit the driver's door handle and dropped as the gun barrel rose to the window and belched flame.

The glass imploded, spraying the interior of the car with cubes of crystal. Bolan's reflexes, honed to razor edge keenness by a lifetime in the killing grounds, were that vital hundredth of a second faster than the assassin's. The soldier had the door open and was already pitching down and out while the killer's trigger finger tightened.

The hot breath of the deathbringer fanned his cheek as he fell but Bolan was untouched.

He shoulder-rolled on the asphalt and came up crouching beside the BMW's front wheel. His Beretta 93-R was already out of its underarm rig and seeking a target.

Bolan peered beneath the vehicle and saw the killer's feet skating around the front of the car. The warrior unleashed a 3-round burst, and then another, the blasts deafening in the confined space beneath the hot engine.

There was a scream of pain and the thump of a falling body as one of the 9 mm slugs shattered an ankle.

But the gunman had thrown himself down behind the raised concrete platform on which the pumps stood...and now there was a second voice shouting, and more footsteps pounding toward the BMW from the refreshment counter.

Bolan eased himself away from the wheel, then ran, crouching, for the next row of pumps. He dived for cover once more as the newcomer opened fire. Cement chips stung the Executioner's face. There was a tinkle of falling glass from the pump's savaged dials. And now cold, aromatic liquid gurgled across the back of his hand: gasoline was splashing from the broken viewer at the top of the hose.

The second man was holding a compact submachine gun—Bolan guessed it was a mini-Uzi—strafing the pump area with hot lead as he approached.

There were ten rows of pumps ranked beneath the station canopy, in staggered formation to accommodate heavy vacation traffic. Bolan's BMW was parked in the fourth line; the Executioner himself was crouched behind the fifth. He emptied the magazine of the auto-loader and ran for the sixth, scrambling between pumps and over the platform. If he was lucky, maybe he could hold them off until the next customer drove in for gas.

Maybe.

He glanced toward the access strip leading from the expressway.

Bolan frowned. A cord with small triangular flags was strung across the entrance to the rest area.

There had been no cord when Bolan arrived.

That meant they had been waiting for him. It also meant that there was a third killer at large. The guy who had positioned those flags would be on his way to join the battle. And unless Bolan moved now he would be enfiladed.

Behind him there were four more rows of pumps, and then a strip of hardtop bordering a shrub-covered bank that separated the station from the expressway. He slammed a fresh magazine into the Beretta.

The thug with the shattered ankle was firing from the far side of the BMW. The hardman with the Uzi was up and running. Bolan waited until the gunner was almost beneath the canopy, braced his weapon in the classic shooting stance and dropped the killer with a 3-round punch.

The third man was approaching now. His silhouette was lost against the dark mass of shrubbery, but Bolan could hear his footsteps swishing through long grass. Maybe thirty yards away.

Bolan raced toward the seventh row...the eighth...the ninth. Panting, he dropped behind the concrete ledge. He had to make those bushes before Number Three was within accurate target range.

Halfway to his feet, he froze. A big sedan with no lights was crawling into view from behind the candy shop.

Bolan was momentarily stymied. He had not counted on any reinforcements for the hit team. He dismissed it, as another question crowded his mind.

Were they waiting for The Executioner...or for Kurt Sondermann, the dead German he was impersonating?

It had to be the hit man, Bolan thought. A helicopter had ferried him from Interpol headquarters in Geneva to the place where the German had been killed. But even if anyone had known Bolan was in Geneva, had seen him board the chopper, there was no way they could have ferreted out its destination.

And unless the Interpol chief or the French Counterintelligence man were tied in with the Mob, there was no way anyone could have guessed at the Executioner's involvement.

On the other hand, Chamson and Telder had known of the hit man's plans, so perhaps others closer to his own line of business could have been equally well briefed.

Sondermann's BMW had run off the road at 100 plus miles per hour, the Swiss and French lawmen had told Bolan. The German had been thrown clear of the blazing wreck, killed instantly. In his pocket, there was a reservation confirming a two-day stopover at a motel outside Lyons. Bolan—provided with a similar car, Sondermann's license plates, and the dead man's papers—had taken up the second of those days.

The Executioner spent a moment reasoning out how the killers had known which gas station the BMW would stop at the following night on its way south.

They knew the car and its fuel capacity. So, it was simple to estimate roughly where the BMW would need to refuel. The filling stations on the expressways were between ten and twenty miles apart, as a rule. If the killers covered three they should be ninety percent certain to catch the BMW.

So, sure, it all made sense to the soldier. What did not make sense was why they were so anxious to keep Kurt Sondermann away from Marseilles.

Right now, Bolan had no time to squander on guessing games.

The sedan had stopped on the far side of the canopy, out of effective range for the Beretta. Bolan was familiar with the pattern. Once the guy coming up through the bushes was in position, the car would move forward again, high beams lancing the darkness. Anyone caught in the open would be pinned against the night, as effectively as a moth on a display board, target for a hail of death hosing in from three directions.

It was even more vital now that he quit the shelter of the last row of pumps and find cover in the bushes.

Suddenly the wind started to blow again. It was a typical mistral—one minute still as death, the next, rushing at full bore, flattening the grasses. Bolan took advantage of the abrupt change.

This time he fired no warnings to keep the opposition heads down. He was on his feet and running, dodging, racing for the safety of that bank as a fusillade roared out behind him, ripping apart the night with their hellfire din.

Slugs scuffed the macadam to left and right and punctured pumps in the final row. At the last moment, a bullet took away the heel of Bolan's shoe, to send him hurtling forward on hands and knees.

The fall saved his life: a murderous volley fanned the air above him as he fell, the deathstream savaging the space he'd occupied a moment before. He remained prone on the hard ground, bellying rapidly toward the bushes.

He was in the shrubbery now, branches and leaves threshing angrily above him, breathless in the shadows beneath the howling wind.

With blinding brilliance the headlights swamped the neon beneath the canopy. A voice from behind the car shouted instructions. There was a brief reply from farther along the bank. The gunman approaching from the access strip was now as vulnerable to Bolan's fire as the soldier was to the sedan. The hardman would be worming his way toward the Executioner at ground level.

The Beretta 93-R was Bolan's favorite shoulder-rig weapon. It was also, Telder had told him, the gun usually carried by Kurt Sondermann. To keep in character, Bolan was therefore armed with the pistol recovered from the German's dead body.

The German hit man's Beretta sported the front handgrip that folded beneath the barrel and could be used to steady the gun and minimize the rise in accurate firing. Now that he had a little more time to think, Bolan figured he could use it. Something he had seen glinting on the station forefront in the lights of the sedan had given him an idea.

From beneath the gas-station canopy a slight grade led toward the exit strip, and a thin rivulet of the volatile fuel, reflecting in the harsh illumination, was trickling slowly down the slope.

The sedan was moving again. It was halfway across the staggered rows of pumps, veering from side to side as the headlamp beams swept the shrub-covered bank.

Bolan folded down the foregrip and wrapped the fingers of his left hand around it. The Beretta's butt nestled in his right palm, and the index was curled around the trigger.

Prone in the shadows, he leaned on his elbows and sighted carefully. He thumbed the auto-catch and put a couple of 3-round bursts in a tight pattern at the base of a pump. The spirit gushed out; from where he lay he could smell the odor of the fuel.

The light beams had jerked his way when the shots rang out. Now livid flashes winked from the driver's window.

Heavy slugs ripped through the branches above him. The sound of the burst was muffled, snatched away by the wind.

Bolan rolled farther down the bank, crouched behind a larger bush. For the moment, he had to forget the killer who would be trying to enfilade him: he needed all his concentration for the task at hand.

The mistral screeched through dry stalks and sang in the wires somewhere overhead, that fed electricity to the station. Occasionally headlamp beams from traffic on the expressway swept through the foliage, but the sound of the engines was lost in the wind.

Bolan waited.

Gasoline from the drilled pump had flooded out to flow down the grade. He could see the vapor shimmering above it in the glare from the approaching sedan. Back on single-shot action, he sighted the Beretta between the car's front wheels and squeezed the trigger.

The slug plowed into the moist macadam. He crouched lower, flattening the trajectory, fired again. A ricochet. The car's radiator grill was a yard from the high-octane gas flow.

Bent lower still, straining his eyes, Bolan held his breath and coaxed a third shot from the 93-R. This time the heavy slug, traveling almost parallel to the tarmac, homed in on one of the flints surfacing in the worn matrix of the macadam.

The round glanced off the stone and thunked into the underside of the vehicle, leaving a spark behind it.

The spark jumped into the inflammable vapor rising from the spreading gasoline.

The whole sweep of gasoline ignited with an explosion that rocked the ground as the sedan passed over it.

Instantly, the car was transformed into a blazing fire-ball. The pump that Bolan had holed went up with a roar. Flames flattened, teased out, driven by the wind, reached white-hot fingers around other damaged pumps and squeezed smoke, then fire, from their shells. Out of the holocaust that had been the sedan, a blackened scarecrow figure seething with tongues of flame flopped screaming onto the pavement.

Within seconds the whole area beneath the canopy was an inferno. From the center of the fiery maelstrom there was a colossal explosion as an underground tank blew. The concrete roofing collapsed and flames boiled skyward, pillowing a huge column of black smoke.

Bolan's eyebrows, lashes and hair were singed by the furious heat. The killer from the car now lay motionless with smoke and steam wisping from his charred body.

Bolan scrambled around to face the slope rising from the rest area. The last assassin was someplace there among the dancing shadows between the bushes.

The Beretta's first magazine had been emptied and nine shots had already sneezed out from the 15-round spare. Expecting no trouble before he reached Marseilles, Bolan had carried no more. He would have to be damned sure of his target if the last six rounds were to get him out of here.

Another smaller detonation cracked out from the far side of the blaze. He guessed the fumes in the empty tank of his BMW had erupted.

Lit by the leaping flames, the bushy slope was a chaos of flying shadows and branches tossed by the gale.

When the first shot came, it was from a point nearer down the bank than Bolan had expected. He heard nothing over the moan of the wind, saw only a pale twinkle of fire stabbing the shadows among the redder reflections of the flames.

A stream of lead from an SMG on full-auto thwacked through the branches above Bolan's head. Twigs and leaves fluttered down around him. A sudden gust blew them away across the bank. The killer saw the movement and fired again.

Aiming above the muzzle-flashes, Bolan sacrificed a couple of rounds, but the light was deceptive and this time he didn't score.

Four shells left in the magazine.

Now the invisible gunman was nearer, perhaps no more than twenty yards away. Bolan ducked and rolled once more to a new position.

There was a long burst, uncomfortably close.

Bolan uttered a realistic cry of pain and sprawled, still in shadow, on his back. He snicked the Beretta to 3-shot mode. The Executioner was counting on the carelessness born of confidence, something he had seen happen to the enemy many times in Vietnam: not making sure of the kill. Suddenly, Bolan realized that he was dealing with a professional.

Because the killer was running toward him. But it did not necessarily mean that the guy wanted to finish him off. Maybe they had orders to take Sondermann alive.

No matter. The gunner was playing the Executioner's kind of game.

There was a clatter of loose stones and a sudden rush of feet as a dark silhouette materialized, dashing down the slope to leap on Bolan's barely visible body.

The guy was suddenly in mid-air, flailing the SMG like a club.

Bolan drew up his knees. As the killer plummetted toward him, the Executioner impacted his heels in the man's belly and kicked out ferociously.

The guy emitted a yell of astonishment and fear as he flew up over Bolan's head. While he was airborne, a cart-wheeling target against the roaring flames, Bolan raised the Beretta and caressed the trigger.

One of the shots drilled the hood's shoulder, one screamed into the sky, the third took away the top of the man's head.

The impact of the 9 mm parabellum spun him sideways and he crashed into the branches behind Bolan.

Still clutching the 93-R, Bolan stood and ran toward the candy store behind the raging fire.

He had to leave fast. A couple of semis and several cars had already pulled up at the entrance to the rest area, and there was a small crowd of rubberneckers advancing toward the flags.

He skirted the raging fire and approached the store. The lights had gone but the structure was intact. Bolan peered over the counter.

The attendant lying there had been shot in the neck. The body of a second man, stripped of its coverall, had been dragged farther back, beneath the soft-drink dispensers. There was nothing Bolan could do for either of them.

He figured his best plan would be to climb the fence sealing off the rest area and strike out cross-country until he came to a highway. It would be easier to find transport—and risk fewer questions—than a return to the expressway.

He was hurrying away from the building when he heard a faint cry over the crackle of the flames.

He looked over his shoulder and saw something moving between him and the fire. He moved closer. It was the man with the shattered ankle. Bolan had assumed he'd been incinerated when the gasoline ignited, but he had managed to drag himself fifty yards beyond the blaze.

The guy was in a bad way. The flesh that showed through gaps in his charred clothing was puffed and blistered with third-degree burns.

As Bolan stooped over him the eyes turned his way and the ruined mouth opened. "Finish it, please," the injured man croaked.

"Who sent you?" Bolan asked.

"Screw you," the hood whispered.

Bolan was holding the Beretta in his right hand. He started to releather the weapon.

"No!" the gunman said frantically. "Please...all right, damn you, Scotto sent us."

"Scotto's dead," Bolan said roughly.

"Aren't we all?" The voice was faint now, showing no curiosity. "We got our orders a week ago. Let you have it someplace between...Lyons and the...coast."

"Why?"

The eyes looked up pleadingly. Bolan waited, his gun hand arrested halfway to the holster.

"He was...afraid," the burned man gasped. "He...figured you for...J-P's answer to...splinter group..."

J-P, Bolan knew, stood for Jean-Paul, the Unione Corse's big wheel in Marseilles, and the man who had hired Sondermann. If he had a family name it was never used. "What splinter group? Where?" Bolan demanded.

The blackened head rolled from side to side. The hood gave a strangled scream. When next he spoke, his voice was so low that Bolan could barely catch the words.

"Meeting..." he choked. "Tomorrow night...at La R-R-Rocaille..."

The words lapsed into an incoherent mumble punctuated by gasps of agony. Bolan was going to get no more from him.

The face contorted. Froth appeared between the cracked lips.

There was a single bullet left in the Beretta. Bolan pointed the muzzle at the center of the dying man's forehead and triggered a mercy round.

3

"Maybe I'm the ultimate optimist," Mack Bolan had once written in his journal. "I believe my sword hand is guided by thoughts of victory. I command myself to win. Therefore, I have the advantage."

The advantage, yeah. But too often in his everlasting war, the hellfire warrior had to forge that advantage in the flames of overwhelming disadvantage.

Bolan was no superman. He knew the limits of his abilities. And he also knew that at any moment a stray, indeed a well-placed bullet, could finish him in the hellgrounds. The thought made him frustrated and anxious because he sensed a growing possibility of victory by the dark forces of the world.

Bolan believed that the savages, the evil legions of animal man, should not be allowed to inherit the earth. The Executioner considered their defeat his vocation. He was prepared to sacrifice love, a home life, a normal career, everything to fight those legions, and if possible to halt the advance of evil man so that gentle civilizers would no longer live in fear. And every ounce of his soldier's resolution was dedicated to that cause.

Learning his deadly skills in the jungles of Vietnam, Bolan had subsequently, in the murderous one-man war that virtually destroyed the Mafia, transferred those skills to the urban jungles of his homeland.

Later, there had been the antiterrorist crusade, fought with covert government approval from Stony Man Farm, a fortress headquarters in Virginia's Blue Ridge Mountains. As Colonel John Phoenix, he had in this phase of his life escalated his efforts into open war with the KGB. And it was this sinister arm of Soviet oppression that had stage-managed the demolition of the Stony Man operation and the frame-up that had made Bolan an outlaw.

It was as a loner, therefore, a supreme warrior who knew that each victory only brought him face-to-face with a new threat, that Bolan had been coopted for the present campaign.

So he understood now why Telder, Chamson and their superiors had chosen him. If the deal went sour for Bolan, they would not be responsible and they'd have nothing to worry about. Because he was an outlaw on just about every continent. If something big was planned and Bolan stopped it…well, they'd simply smile and relax, reap the honors. In any case, Telder and Chamson would come out of it with clean hands.

Okay, if that was the way the cards were dealt, he'd play the hand.

His mandate was to uncover the "something big" that was being planned in the Riviera underworld, to find out what black conspiracy was being hatched in the cold minds of the men running that crime empire.

Before he ventured on the inside, where his movements might not be as free as he wished, he determined to follow up the only lead he had: a few strange words choked from the scorched lips of a dying goon.

A meeting was about to take place. And it was, according to the burned hardman's last words, important, to be held somewhere called La Rocaille.

Bolan was experiencing a gut reaction that it was important for him to be around when that happened.

Once in Marseilles, Bolan wasted no time. He knew precisely who would give him the information he needed.

He entered a noisy bar on the Canebière. "La Rocaille?" the swarthy man behind the counter repeated. "Sure. It's the old Delamour joint, on the coast between here and Cassis."

Bolan took a cab. La Rocaille was an islet, no more than two hundred yards offshore, below jagged cliffs separating the city from the famous little fishing port. There were a couple of acres of undulating ground above the limestone wall surrounding the islet, and here, sheltered by tall hedges and set in a cypress grove, an extraordinary building had been erected.

It was a huge house, built on several different levels, combining gothic turrets with Oriental domes above a fantasy of Moorish arches and windows.

"Who owns it?" Bolan inquired.

"It was built by Deborah Delamour, the silent screen star of the twenties," the cabbie said. "After her death, the property remained empty until the mid-sixties. It was bought recently and restored by an industrialist named Sanguinetti."

"Are visitors allowed?" Bolan asked conversationally.

"Are you kidding?" the cab driver replied. "Sanguinetti's got guard dogs, closed-circuit TV, electrified fences, you name it." He gestured across the stretch of calm blue water. "In Delamour's time, there used to be a suspension bridge, but that's the only way you can get there now."

He was indicating a small concrete jetty projecting from the base of the cliff on the landward side of the islet. Steps cut from the rock zigzagged to the top of the limestone face, and there was what looked like a cable car rail, with an open car, rising directly from the jetty.

A white power launch was tied next to the steps, with two burly men wearing blue sailors' jerseys lounging nearby. Another guard stood by a tall wrought-iron gateway at the top of the stairway. "No beaches on the other side of the island?" Bolan asked.

The taxi driver shook his head. "Sheer cliffs all the way around," he said.

Bolan glanced right and left. The heat had gone from the sun, but there were still vacationers bronzing themselves on the sandy strip below the road. Kids swam in the shallows, and there were half a dozen windsurfers offshore, waiting for a breeze.

Beyond a line of automobiles parked on a low bluff, he could see striped umbrellas and a beach restaurant at the inner end of a pleasure pier. A thicket of sailboat masts clustered around the wooden piles. "They use that pier?" Bolan asked.

"Uh-uh. They got a regular service of those floating bars—" he nodded toward the launch "—bringing them out, sometimes from the city, mostly from Cassis."

Bolan nodded, as if dismissing the subject but the whole area intrigued him. Boatloads of people were ferried from Cassis to a heavily guarded property owned by an industrialist, and there was to be an important secret meeting...more than ever Bolan determined to smuggle himself onto that islet. "Okay, let's go to Cassis now," he told the driver.

The village was five miles away, around a bend in the cliffs, but to get there the road circled behind some wild rocky slopes. Sanguinetti sure had picked himself an isolated retreat, Bolan reflected.

Bolan paid the cabbie, rented a Volkswagen and drove down to the dockside. From a ship's chandler store he rented scuba equipment, a waterproof neoprene satchel and a spear gun. Then he drove back toward Marseilles and down to the coastal road, which petered out a few hundred yards beyond the bluff where he had stopped the taxi.

At the end of the road, he concealed the VW behind an immense boulder and returned to the bluff on foot. He changed into the diving suit, strapped on the oxygen tank, drew on helmet and facemask and stowed the Beretta in the satchel. Picking up the flippers and his spear gun, he moved toward the water's edge.

The night was very warm. The three-quarter moon was not due to silver the cloudless sky for another hour. The sea was calm. Bolan stepped into the flippers and waded in.

Several boats had already chugged out from Cassis to Sanguinetti's jetty. He could see the riding lights bobbing at the base of the cliff. Voices and laughter drifted across the water, and there was a hint of music from the house above.

Bolan submerged and swam slowly and steadily toward the small island, using a luminous waterproof wrist compass to maintain direction. The sea became progressively colder as he approached the islet. There were deeps along this stretch of coast and the fissured limestone let in many small creeks, one of which he hoped to find on the seaward side of Sanguinetti's fortress.

Fifteen minutes after he had entered the water, Bolan surfaced. He was west of the property, about thirty yards out from the cliff. There was a swell here that had not been evident from the shore; he could hear the suck of the waves as they lapped against the rocks.

He continued swimming. When the dark mass of the island was between him and the shore, he turned east and struck out on the surface for the limestone face.

He could see no sign of an opening in the sheer rock wall.

Although the tide fall was minimal, a strong current ruled out any close approach to the cliff: if he swam in and tried to locate a foothold from which he could climb to the top, he risked injury on some underwater obstruction or being dashed against one of the jagged outcroppings. Treading water, he allowed the tide to carry him farther toward the east.

When he could see the mainland again, he turned once more and made for the cliffs.

There were two creeks in the eastern face.

From the shore, the farthest was little more than a gash in the limestone. Bolan dismissed it at once: the walls bordering the creek were almost as high as the cliff itself, and in some places they overhung the water.

The second was better. The strata dipped, plunged beneath the surface, leaving a narrow inlet, from whose inner end the rock rose steeply but was not sheer.

Bolan thought he could make the climb. The disadvantage was that he had almost completed a circuit of the island: the creek was shielded from the jetty by a single shoulder of limestone.

He had come too far to turn back. Besides, the shuttle service from Cassis seemed to have stopped. No more guests climbed the stairway or were whisked aloft by the cable car. Only the two burly guards from the launch remained talking there. Bolan would have to take a chance, scaling the slope with as little noise as possible. Fortunately, there was still music and occasional laughter drifting down.

Bolan floated, letting himself be washed into the creek by the waves. At the shallow end he rose cautiously, allowing the seawater to cascade from his wet suit as gently as he could.

Rock climbing in darkness is hazardous at the best of times, and tonight any trace of daylight lingering in the western sky was blocked by the mass of the island itself. He grasped a projection, a layer of harder rock that formed a thin shelf, and started to haul himself up the slope.

It took what seemed an eternity and innumerable teeth-gritting seconds of his determination to make the stealthy ascent. Once or twice small fragments of limestone broke off under the pressure of his fingers or toes and rattled to the water below. Once his foot slipped and he almost fell. But the small sounds of the sea appeared to have covered the noise, for there was no reaction from the far side of the rock shoulder; the voices from the jetty did not pause in their low-toned conversation.

Finally Bolan gained the flat ground at the top of the cliffs. The grotesque mass of the house lay directly ahead, on the far side of some tropical shrubbery. The music was louder now, and there was a dim luminescence reflected from some outside light around a corner of the building.

Waiting, he saw that there were indeed guards patrolling the grounds, but he neither saw nor heard any dogs. If there were sensors installed, the guards either knew to the inch the right path to take between the beams or they were equipped with desensitizer pads, for no alarm was sounded.

Finally, Bolan discarded the flippers that had been slung around his neck, picked up the spear gun and moved silently after one man, following exactly in his tracks.

He was almost at an ornamental terrace when another guy, a bruiser whose height dwarfed Bolan's own six foot three, stepped out from behind a bank of oleanders and barred his way.

The confrontation, as sudden as it was unexpected, astonished both men equally. The guard, who was wearing a black turtleneck sweater over jeans, was holding a Heckler & Koch 9-6 automatic. Seeing the dark, helmeted figure of the Executioner, squarely in front of him, wet suit still gleaming in the reflected light, he brought up the gun instinctively.

There was no time for Bolan to unfasten the neoprene satchel and whip out the Beretta. Hand-to-hand combat was unthinkable with the gorilla's finger already curling around the trigger. Bolan was carrying the spear gun at port. He had no time to sight the weapon. At arm's length he canted up the long, thin launch tube and fired.

A heartbeat before the gunman's finger squeezed tight, the steel-barbed tip of the harpoon took him in the throat.

Arrowing in with terrible force, the razor-sharp head sliced through the jugular vein, flattened the ridges of the trachea and severed the carotid artery. The barb forced an exit to one side of the topmost cervical vertebra and left the shaft stuck in the gorilla's savaged neck. He fell, clawing at his throat, and died.

Bolan dragged the body away to the cliff top and dropped it, together with the spear gun, into a crevice.

He turned the corner of the house, the Beretta now in his right hand. He was facing a sunken rock garden. Behind it, light escaped from windows under an arched colonnade. Through the windows he could see women in evening gowns walking back and forth. Apart from a white-coated waiter with a tray of drinks, no men were visible.

Hugging the shadows, Bolan crossed the garden, skirted a wing of the building and found himself on an open balustraded terrace that overlooked an Olympic-size pool. He was halfway across the terrace, threading his way between glass topped tables and lounging chairs, when he heard footsteps crunch on gravel.

He looked swiftly around. No place to hide here. He vaulted the balustrade, crossed a strip of flagstones and lowered himself silently into the shallow end of the pool.

He kept his head just above the surface and now he heard footsteps approaching, halt too near the corner of the pool where he was half submerged.

"Frank?" the guard called in a low voice. "You there?"

There was no reply.

The man shouted again, louder this time.

Bolan's thoughts were racing. This guard must have a rendezvous...with the gorilla he had harpooned.

Bolan no longer had any compunction. This was no honest millionaire's summer party. The first guard's readiness to kill proved that. Bolan rose and reached for the guard's ankle.

Hearing the swirl of water, the guy swung around. Before his eyes could register in the dark, Bolan's steely fingers closed around flesh and bone. He heaved. Caught off balance, the guard staggered, almost fell.

Bolan jerked again, harder. The man flew over his head and belly flopped into the pool.

Bolan was on him before he had time to turn onto his back or surface. The guard struggled desperately.

The pool became a maelstrom of foam and thrashing limbs. Bolan had the advantage of surprise and superior strength. The guard was holding a gun, but right now his overriding desire was for self-preservation...his need for air, to feed his bursting lungs.

Bolan found his wrist, applied a nerve grip, forcing him to drop the weapon. Remorselessly he forged through the water, shoving the drowning guard toward the deep end.

Finally Bolan maneuvered the hardman to the side, where a ladder led back up to the flagstone patio. He hooked his arms over the top of the ladder while he thrust down with his feet to keep his victim submerged until at last the frantic struggles weakened and then ceased.

Bolan left the body floating facedown in the pool, recovered the Beretta from where he had dropped it on the terrace, and hurried back to the house. He turned another corner and looked across sloping lawns to a hedge over which the distant lights of the city made a faint glow in the sky.

The ground rose here, leaving a railed area circling the building. Bolan looked down through the top half of tall windows to a large paneled room in the center of which eleven men sat around a boardroom table. He caught his breath. So, this must be the "important" meeting.

Crouching, he saw that the room was surrounded by a gallery. A short flight of steps led to a door that was clearly an entrance to this gallery.

At the top of the stairs he tried the door. It was not locked. A fraction of an inch at a time, he eased open the door, waited, pushed lightly. The door swung silently inward and he slipped through.

Carved wooden balusters railed in the gallery, which was in deep shadow. The room below was lit by three green-shaded lamps that hung, poolroom style, over the vast table. Bolan lowered himself to the floor and peered down between two balusters.

A big ornate chair at the head of the table was empty. Sanguinetti, the owner of the property—Bolan recognized him from newspaper photos—was installed at the foot. The other ten men were ranged five on either side.

They were talking among themselves. Bolan could make out no individual words, could hear no names. But he did not have to. He realized he was looking at ten of the most powerful men in the world.

And the most evil.

Facing him beneath the low-hanging poolroom lamps, Bolan saw the rock-hard features of Vincente Borrone, whose family controlled docks and transport Stateside; Luigi Abba, the undisputed boss of Vegas and the West Coast; the Unione Corse capo, Renato Ancarani; Arturo Zefarelli from Sicily; and Pasquale Lombardo, who ran the Mob in Toulon.

For a while Bolan was unable to pinpoint the crime emperors with their backs to him, but the conversation around the table was animated, and eventually each had turned toward a neighbor sufficiently for the Executioner to pedigree the other five.

The first he recognized was Girolamo Scalese, king of the Camorra in Naples.

Next to him was the Baron Etang de Brialy, a small gray-haired Frenchman with gold-rimmed eyeglasses, who was the Mister Big behind all organized crime in Paris. Between this couple and Sanguinetti were two hoods whose names Bolan could not remember but who controlled, he knew, the Mafia in Chicago and Detroit. The quorum was completed by Jean-Paul.

It was the first time Bolan had seen the Marseilles gang leader in the flesh, and he looked at the man with interest.

J-P was impressive. He was a big guy, almost as tall as Bolan, and appeared to be in his early forties. He was trim, bronzed, the sharp planes of his face etched with laugh-lines, his head unexpectedly capped with thick white hair.

Bolan smiled wryly. If he had known his future "employer" would be at the meeting he probably could have entered the fortress openly and even been invited as a guest. As it was, he would have to get out fast before the absence of the two men he had killed was noticed. He couldn't afford to have Sondermann associated with that.

But first, he wanted to find out the purpose of the meeting. Nothing was happening right now: the eleven men appeared to be waiting for something. Or someone.

A few minutes later, Bolan heard the clattering whine of an approaching jet helicopter. The noise increased and then it subsided as the chopper landed somewhere on the far side of the pool.

A whistle sounded. Almost immediately the aircraft took off again and flew out to sea.

As the rotor whine faded in the distance, conversation in the room below the gallery dwindled too. A door opened; a voice made an announcement.

A thickset man with a shaven skull marched into the room, nodded briefly and took the vacant chair at the head of the table.

Bolan choked back a gasp of astonishment.

The man was in military uniform; he wore the insignia of a Colonel in the Red Army.

His name, Bolan knew, was Dimitri Aleksandrevitch Antonin. And the last time they had met, Bolan had shot him in the shoulder and left him for dead. So, the liaison between the KGB and the Soviet military intelligence agency, the GRU, was still alive.

4

Bolan didn't get it. On one of his daring one-man raids into Soviet Russia, Colonel Antonin had been in charge of the manhunt ordered at all costs to stop him from leaving the country with a defecting scientist.

At that time, Antonin had been assistant to Major General Greb Strakhov, the evil genius of the KGB responsible for the frame that had outlawed Bolan. He wondered now if Antonin had taken Strakhov's place as head of the KGB's "wet affairs" death squad. Or if he had returned to his original post as KGB-GRU liaison under the department's Third Chief Directorate.

Moscow was a hell of a long way from Southern France. And what was he doing here chairing a meeting of international racketeers?

Whatever it was, the Executioner knew, it would be something as corrupt as it was illegal.

He craned his neck trying to hear every word exchanged around the long table below. The conversation, which had been in French, had now lapsed into an English with more varieties of accent than Bolan had ever heard in one place.

"You know why I am here," Antonin said curtly. "It is a matter for you to decide among yourselves—here, now, and I want a decision before I leave—whether you are prepared to accept my offer."

Bolan's eyes opened wide. He was eavesdropping on some evil scheme that the KGB was anxious to promote, that was clearly going to link crime with sedition.

"Very well, Colonel," Jean-Paul was saying, "we are aware of the general strategy. Now let us hear the details."

"They are not complicated," Antonin replied. "You and the elements you represent are locked in permanent combat with the law, both nationally and internationally. Is it not so?"

He paused. "I am not," he continued, "concerned here with questions of so-called morality, with the bourgeois-imperialist concepts of good and evil, right or wrong. In my country we subscribe to the doctrine that victory goes to the strongest, that might, as you Westerners have it, is right. I make, therefore, no value judgments in assessing your particular role in your society. I view it objectively." Another, longer, pause. "And objectively speaking, you are weak."

Several of the mafiosi shifted uneasily at Antonin's words. Weak? That was the last term they would apply to themselves. They were the emperors of crime, and people lived or died according to their orders.

Scalese, the Camorra boss, muttered something under his breath to Renato Ancarani. The New York capo, Borrone, scowled and only just managed to check a heated reply that sprang to his lips.

"You are weak," Antonin repeated, thumping the table, "because you are always in an inferior position relative to your lawmakers. However important the scale of your operations, you are scared of the law."

He held up his hand as the murmurs of dissent around the table rose to an angry climax.

"I am not questioning your personal courage. My criticism is aimed at the position from which you mount those operations. And no reasoned analysis of the current situation could characterize your position as anything but weak.''

In the gloom of the gallery above, Mack Bolan grinned. The hoods were being fed home truths…and they didn't like it.

Antonin pressed on relentlessly. "What I am offering is the means to reverse this situation. If you accept the offer, soon *you* will be in the driving seat; the law and its enforcement officers will be scared of *you*.''

"And just how,'' Toulon's Pasquale Lombardo rasped, "do we get to be that way?''

"Your present inferior position,'' Antonin said, "is largely a matter of logistics. That plus a lack of coordinated command and a generalized resistance on the part of the public.''

"Oh, yeah?'' This was Borrone, and he clearly did not understand Antonin's words. "And how the fuck do you figure we could change all that?''

"An unlimited supply of arms,'' the Russian said calmly. "We cannot, of course, be directly involved, but I can arrange for Omnipol, the official Czech arsenal, to furnish you with Kalashnikov AK-74s, Tokarev and Stechkin automatics, Skorpion machine pistols, explosives, RPG-7 grenade launchers, ground-to-ground guided missiles, anything you want.

"With the firepower these sophisticated weapons will give you—especially if they are in unlimited quantity—you will have the police running for cover any time you choose to show your faces.''

"Shit, I ain't buyin' that,'' Arturo Zefarelli said. "Even with that amount of heat, the different goddamn families'll never—''

"Ah, but there is a corollary,'' Antonin cut in.

"Come again?"

"A condition without which it's no deal. Naturally we do not make such an offer without the hope of some...recompense."

"Here it comes," Ancarani whispered to Scalese. "The fucking bite!"

"Our interest," Antonin said, "is in the destabilization of Western society. You know that, of course. I am assuming that none of you...disapproves." The sneer in his voice was evident. "No? Very well, then. I will add that we believe this society carries within it the seeds of its own destruction. The existence of organizations such as yours proves the point. But we wish to hasten the process so that communism can take over more rapidly."

The KGB officer sat back in his chair and laid his hands on the table. "Our other efforts have had a limited success. And I am speaking of our support for the so-called extremist or terrorist groups, mainly among the Arabs, the Armenians and the Irish. But it is all too minor—too slow. That is why we have come to you. Properly organized and armed, you could wreak havoc with the world as the capitalists have ordered it. I emphasize: properly organized."

"Meaning?"

"Meaning that even with the arms, I suggest you would remain a loosely connected but disparate *collection* of units. What we want is a single integrated group. The offer, therefore, is conditional on your establishing one individual worldwide crime syndicate, entirely disciplined, and obeying orders from a single central command."

"Which you would wish to control?" Jean-Paul asked.

"Not control," Colonel Antonin said suavely. "We should be pleased to offer advice."

"Okay, so what's in it for us?" the gang leader from Detroit demanded.

"For you there would be rewards a thousand times greater than anything you have achieved so far. But first you *must* unify."

"So what happens when the society's fucked over and the Reds move in? I mean, what happens to us?" Luigi Abba said sourly. "I mean, I don't see no Syndicate cathouses or dope rings or numbers games in your friggin' commie paradise. Me, I don't fancy no salt mine detail."

"It is not a problem that is likely to arise for some time. Even if our project succeeds." Antonin's smile was bland. "In any case, room can always be found for men of enterprise and initiative."

Etang de Brialy, the Parisian, spoke for the first time. "This flood of arms you so generously offer," he said mildly, "just how will it be paid for?"

"Not with money, if that is what worries you," Antonin replied. "Let us say by the rendering of certain special services."

"Such as?"

The Russian did not reply directly. "You have a system, I believe," he said, "for the removal of unwanted individuals. Well, from time to time we shall feed *you* contract jobs that call for the liquidation of elements embarrassing to us. Labor leaders, diplomats, an occasional politician. Maybe a journalist whose views we find uncomfortable. People with whose disposal we must on no account be directly connected. The success of such operations will amply reward my superiors for any...logistic help...they can supply."

Flat on his face in the gallery, Bolan could feel his heart pounding against his ribs. This was the conspiracy "brewing in the Riviera underworld" that Telder and Chamson had suspected.

The KGB were now planning to recruit the entire Mafia brotherhood worldwide. They were deliberately marshaling the forces of crime to further their own despotic ambitions.

Bolan was under no illusion as to the threat a global KGB-Mafia partnership would pose. With the means at their disposal, and the whole weight of the Soviet Union secretly behind them, they could—as Antonin prophesied—drive democracy to the wall.

He wondered if the hoods below could see things equally clearly; if they were dumb enough to believe that the KGB would allow them to direct their own organization once they had accepted Russian aid.

Bolan himself knew damned well what would happen. Once the Mob had accepted the KGB handout, they would simply become reinforcements to the seven hundred thousand agents already implementing Moscow's plans all over the world.

Right now, though, Antonin was spoon-feeding them the story that all would be best in the best of possible worlds. Hell, this is all the world needs, Bolan thought savagely.

"Okay, okay," he heard the Chicago gang boss say. "So we make with all these shooters and get the cops running. What if they bring in the army then?"

"Yeah," Borrone said. "Cops with .38 Police Specials or Brownings is one thing; paras with all the gear they have is another."

"The fact that the army might be involved would add to the confusion," Antonin said smoothly. "People would see their world collapsing; they would be traumatized. In any case, you would still have the advantage."

"No kidding!" Zefarelli scoffed. "Just tell me how."

"Simple," said the Russian. "The army would have to be careful to avoid civilian casualties in any shootout. Otherwise the political repercussions would be disastrous. You would work under no such restrictions. The more bystanders shot down the better. Calling in the soldiers is already an admission that the situation is out of hand. Either way we win."

"I don't know," one of the capos said dubiously. "We make enough bread the way things are. Why take a chance and—"

"You would be taking no chances," Antonin interrupted. "But there is no hurry. Talk it over. I shall be here until midnight. Why don't we, uh, join the ladies? You can let me know what you have decided when you have discussed it among yourselves."

A smart time to ease off on the hard sell, Bolan figured. There was a scraping of chairs as the mafiosi stood up. Led by Sanguinetti, they filed, talking heatedly, toward a door leading to the main part of the house. Bolan pushed himself to his hands and knees. Time to split before they found the guards he had zapped.

Now that he knew the score, it would be great if he could somehow patch in to the hoods' decision. He glanced over his shoulder at the garden exit.

And froze.

Eighteen inches from his head there was a pair of glossy black high-heel boots. Above the boots, glove-leather pants and a matching draped jacket clothed a shapely brunette. She held a small blue-steel automatic in her right hand.

"The knockdown power is nonexistent," she said softly. "But at this range, in experienced hands, it can be lethal. And I assure you I am experienced. I think you had better come with me."

5

She wore a flame-colored scarf tucked into the neck of her jacket. Her eyes were green and her hair fell softly about her shoulders. She must be, Bolan guessed, all of twenty-two years old.

She was cautious, never allowing the Executioner close enough to make any attempt to disarm her as she maneuvered him back outside the terrace and then into a small summer house on the far side of the pool.

"Sit on that bench," she said, indicating a seat opposite her, "and tell me why you are eavesdropping on my father's friends." She switched on a pink-shaded light in the wooden roof of the building. "Why you *swam out* here to eavesdrop on my father's friends," she amended, seeing the wet suit and helmet Bolan wore.

Seeing her in the half light of the gallery, he decided she was even prettier than he had thought. "Who is your father?" he countered.

"The owner of the property, of course." She sounded irritated. "I am Coralie Sanguinetti."

"Some friends," Bolan said. He pulled off the rubber helmet. The girl took in the rakish lines of his face, the blue eyes and determined jaw.

"I have to admit you're better looking," she said with the hint of a smile.

He was unclipping the neoprene satchel from his belt. "You don't mind," he began.

"Yes, I do mind." The voice was suddenly hard. "Drop that on the floor....kick it over to me—" She broke off, picking up the satchel. "Just as I thought!"

Keeping her eyes on the Executioner, the little gun steady in her hand, Coralie Sanguinetti unclasped the neoprene container. "A 93-R!" she said. "That's quite a— Wait a minute!" She stared at him again. "I know that face," she said. "I've seen photos. You're J-P's new trigger man, Sondermann. From Hamburg. Am I right?"

"Kurt Sondermann," Bolan said gravely. "At your service, Fräulein."

"You don't sound German." Coralie was puzzled. "You don't have much of an accent."

"In my line of business, it's best to be as inconspicuous as possible. Know what I mean?"

She was still looking doubtful. "But if you are working for Jean-Paul, why do you have to spy on him? Why not come to the front door and say who you are?"

Bolan had an answer ready in case he was discovered by the hoods themselves. "Put the gun away and I'll tell you," he said.

She hesitated, then thumbed the automatic to safety and thrust it into the pocket of her jacket. But she didn't return the Beretta to Bolan; it lay on the bench within easy reach of her right hand.

Smart, he thought. "Some gorillas tried to stop me from getting here. I'd been tailed. I was set up at a gas station on the expressway. I had to shoot my way out."

She remained unconvinced. "So?"

"So I heard there was some kind of a meet on this island. But I'd never heard of your father. I didn't know Jean-Paul was a buddy of his. I figured I'd make it here secretly and find out the score. If it was the same team that tried to waste me, there'd be hell to pay. But as soon as I saw who it was, I knew I had it wrong. I was leaving when you got the drop on me.''

''Who tried to kill you?''

''Guys from an outfit run by someone called Scotto.''

''Oh,'' she said contemptuously. ''Scotto. Anyway, he's dead now.''

''So they tell me. But they didn't tell the guys trying to liquidate me; they didn't know the boss was long gone, so I was nearly dead, too. How come Scotto was killed, anyway?''

''My father told me that J-P and his friends were going into business with...some foreigners. And it seems Scotto and some others didn't like the idea. They wanted to stay the way they were. They were going to get together and...'' She shook her head. ''I don't really know.''

Bolan knew. The pieces were falling into place. Those four murdered mobsters had to be the splinter group. Yeah, that figured. Scotto, Ralfini and the others had been knocked off because they refused to join the ball game. But the KGB offer was contingent on the Mafia chiefs forming a single organization. If four of them were thinking maybe of forming a rival stay-as-you-are group, the Russian offer would be withdrawn.

That explained why the contracts had been put out in a hurry. Any signs of dissension had to be dealt with before Antonin arrived. So that the racketeers could present a front that at least looked united, with no opposition visible.

Bolan frowned. It followed that the mafiosi gathered together in Sanguinetti's house had already made up their minds in principle. Details apart, the KGB-Mafia partnership was on.

He was about to ask the girl what part her father was playing in the scheme when they were both startled by a fusillade from the far side of the house.

Bolan grabbed the Beretta. It sounded like heavy-caliber stuff—9 mm machine pistols or SMGs firing something weightier than the standard 5.56 mm Armalite rounds. "Come on," he rasped. "It sounds as if someone's trying to shoot their way into the party."

Followed by the girl, he sped around the pool and skirted the eastern wing of the house. As he had thought, the gunfire—punctuated now by deeper, heavier reports from single-shot revolvers and the crackle of automatic weapons wielded by the defenders—was concentrated at the head of the stairway leading up from the landing stage.

Reflected light from a gallery bordering the landward side of the house dimly illuminated a paved slope that ran up from the entrance gates to a porch sheltering the main doors. Two formless dark shapes on the porch steps marked the spot where a couple of patrolling guards had fallen. A third lay with outflung arms a few yards from the stair-head gates.

The attackers appeared to be entrenched on the rock steps immediately behind these, on a ledge that traversed the cliff off to one side, and on an open platform of the cable car.

The livid orange and yellow hellfire flashes stabbing the gloom lanced out from these three places and from shrubbery and a storehouse on the far side of the porch. Evidently there were still enough guards alive to prevent the invaders from rushing the house.

But they were too well protected to be picked off one by one, and for anyone trying to get to close quarters, that lethal slope of flagstones meant instant annihilation.

Bolan pulled the girl down behind a row of flowers on the cliff top. Below, in the wan light of a moon that had just risen, he could see the bodies of the two power-launch crewmen stretched out on the stone jetty. A rubber dinghy bobbing beside the white boat showed how the attackers had arrived at the island.

Bolan whispered. "Who are these dudes? Are they gunning for your old man or for his friends?"

"Your guess is as good as mine," Coralie murmured. He saw a white blur of her face turn toward him in the milky light. "Better, perhaps. For all I know..." She left the sentence unfinished.

Bolan was amused. "You think I was some kind of advance guard for these creeps? Think again. I'm on your side—yours and that of those other thugs your dad is hosting."

"Can you prove it?"

"Damn right," Bolan said easily, as he began to move.

On elbows and knees, he pushed his way between the flowers. On the cliff edge he leaned over and gazed toward the stairway.

The killers perched on the rock traverse were invisible in deep shadow now. Beyond them an overhang in the limestone face hid the men on the steps and at the top of the cable. When he and the girl arrived, Bolan had briefly seen bejeweled women huddled behind the windows under the narrow roof of the gallery. Now the lights had all been extinguished, and he could hear the angry voices of the Mafia bosses shouting orders.

The gunfire, which had died away to a sporadic exchange of single shots, broke out again on both sides with renewed fury. Tongues of flame stabbed the darkness from windows on the upper floors of the building. The hidden guards, who seemed to have received reinforcements, redoubled their rate of fire. The attackers raked the facade of the house with a murderous hail of lead.

"Try this way!" Bolan yelled during a lull in the clamor. There was a shout of surprise from the traverse. At once the muzzle-flashes swung his way. Slugs splatted against the rock, ripped through the flower bed and stung his face with stone chips.

Bolan was ready with the Beretta, the folded-down foregrip snug in his left hand. Aiming above the flashes, he let off four 3-shot bursts, the big auto-loader bucking in his hands.

Somebody screamed and fell. A second figure leaned out into the moonlight and dropped, cartwheeling dizzily down the limestone face.

"Enough?" Bolan called to the girl. "Or do you want to make it a trio?"

"Okay, I believe you." She sounded angry again.

Glass shattered on one of the upper stories and a heavy object crashed to the floor inside the house. A woman screamed and a man yelled an obscenity.

Jean-Paul's less hysterical voice called from farther along the facade, "Can't you flush out these bastards, Smiler? There's a meeting we have to finish here."

"Not as long as they stay where they are, J-P," a hoarse voice replied from the storehouse. "We'd be mowed down if we tried to make it across the terrace. You can see—"

The guard called Smiler bit off his words. A fresh volley of automatic fire sounded in the distance, on the eastern side of the house. A second wave of attackers was advancing up the slope from the inlet where Bolan had landed.

The Executioner was still stretched out along the lip of the cliff, the barrel of the Beretta now supported on his left forearm. The gun stuttered the moment the marksmen on the traverse opened up in the direction of Smiler's voice.

An SMG spewed a load of hate uselessly at the sky as another of the killers slammed down on his back, his clothes stitched to his ribs with 9 mm thread.

But now they had located Bolan's position. He was forced to retreat to the other side of a hedge as a savage storm of shot pulverized the limestone where he had been lying.

Shouts now from the far side of the house. The gun-fire—swelled by shooting from the defenders—increased in rapidity and volume. "Your guys in back will be swamped and the dudes on this side taken in the rear and wiped out if we can't waste the squad at the stair head," Bolan said fiercely to Coralie. "That storehouse over there—what's in it?"

"Oh, mostly junk, gardening stuff, chemicals," she said.

"Do they store fuel there?"

"Yes. There's a tank of diesel for the launch, and I think—"

"Diesel's no good. Is there any gasoline?"

"Not much, but we keep a couple of cans for the outboard."

"Can you get to the store? Through the house, without crossing the line of fire? Good. Get me a couple of bottles. Knock off the necks, throw out the wine and replace it with gasoline. Bring them back to me with two corks and some newspaper. Make it fast."

For a moment the girl stared at him uncomprehendingly, then she turned obediently and ran into the dark.

While she was away, Bolan reloaded the Beretta. He was acting in support of the Mafia. That was a laugh. He had spent years of his life successfully eliminating most of that sinister brotherhood in his own country! The soldier shrugged. The thought had occurred to him in the gallery above the conference room that from there a single magazine fired from an Ingram MAC-11, or even a couple of clips from his own Beretta, could wipe out the whole damned roomful and save the world from a new threat. But a massacre of unsuspecting men, even evil ones, was not the Executioner's way.

And again he had wondered, in a brief moment of self-doubt when he and the girl had arrived at the cliff top, if perhaps her suspicions ought not to have been well-founded, if he shouldn't have been helping the attackers rather than the defenders.

Yeah, but that was a question of the devil you knew. And he didn't know who the thugs storming the fortress were. Could be they were even worse than the mafiosi meeting here. There was no way of knowing; better to wait and find out the full extent of the plan masterminded by Antonin before confronting the guys who were to carry it out.

And it was better, for the moment, to remain Kurt Sondermann, arrived on the scene in time to help his new boss.

The girl was beside him again. She held two bottles filled with pinkish fluid and an old newspaper. Bolan sniffed the aromatic odor of gasoline. "I didn't have to break the necks," Coralie said. "There was a stack of empties in the store."

"Good. Did you get the corks?"

She nodded, fishing them out of her jacket pocket and handing them over. Bolan took a bottle, twisted a double sheet of newspaper into a funnel shape, wedged a cork down into the narrowest part and stoppered the bottle so that the paper stood above the neck like a fan. He took a lighter from the neoprene sack.

"What are you doing?" Coralie whispered.

"Wait and see."

He prepared the second bottle in the same way and handed it to the girl.

Using one hand as a shield against the breeze, Bolan flicked the lighter and set fire to the paper above his bottle. He gave the lighter to Coralie. "Light yours and hand it to me as soon as I've tossed mine," he told her.

Blue flames curled the edge of the paper and then the whole mass flared brightly. Boland drew back his arm and hurled the bottle high into the air, toward the stairway.

The girl lit the paper above the second bottle.

Bolan stood. Firing two-handed, he tracked the flaming missile and ripped off a 3-round burst as it began to drop from the sky.

One of the slugs struck home and the bottle exploded. The burning paper ignited gasoline and vapour with a thumping report, showering the hoods on the stone steps with liquid fire.

Bolan reached for the second bottle, lobbed it in a lower trajectory, over the traverse along the cliff. The 93-R chattered again and the bottle disintegrated, igniting the volatile liquid with a dull roar. Once more the night was torn apart with shrieks of pain and panic while the hellfire rain splashed over the trapped gorillas.

Two of them spiraled flaming into the sea. A third clasped scorched hands to the blistered ruin of his face and yelped like a wounded dog. The others beat vainly at their clothes and rolled against the rock in an attempt to extinguish the terrible fire.

It was the same scene on the stairway: writhing bodies, incandescent clothes and hair, animal howls. The guys on the cable-car platform were luckier. Only two of the five men there had been licked by the blazing gasoline and a couple of their comrades manhandled them on the wooden floor, trying to smother the flames.

The last man was on his feet shouting, firing an SMG blindly toward the house. Bolan raised the Beretta, squinted along the sights in the flickering light and dropped him with the last three rounds in the magazine. He tumbled over the edge of the platform and bounced all the way down the rocky slope to the jetty.

Bolan ran out from behind the flowers, calling to the astonished guards hiding in and around the storehouse, "Come on, you guys: all we have to do now is zap those bastards trying to take us from the other side!"

Four or five men in jeans and dark sweaters emerged from the shadows and followed him as he dashed through the shrubbery. There was a crispness, the decisive tone of the born leader, in the Executioner's voice that commanded instant respect and obedience.

But one guy—the guard Jean-Paul had addressed as Smiler—was ready to query Bolan's authority. Smiler came out of the storehouse toting a Smith & Wesson M-76 subgun—a tall, swarthy man with two heavies in tow. "Just a minute, you," he snarled. "Who the fuck you think you are?"

"Sondermann," Bolan said, not pausing in his stride.

"Oh, yeah? Well, I'm the guy gives the orders around here—remember that. Where d'you think you get off, orderin' the boys like some sonovabitch four-star general?"

One of the other men unslung an M-l6 from his shoulder. "Aw, hell, Smiler," he protested, "the dude wasted those punks holed up above the jetty, after all."

"I don't care how many creeps he wasted. I'm still the number-one gun in this neighborhood." He strode after Bolan and tapped him on the shoulder. "You hear me?"

Bolan whirled and seized the front of the hood's sweater in one steely hand, half lifting the hardman off his feet. "No, *you* hear *me*, loudmouth," he growled. "I work alone and I don't aim to take nobody's place. Jean-Paul hired me personally, so I don't reckon to be bugged by no smartass provincial gorilla, understand?"

He thrust Smiler away with force enough to make him stumble.

Choking with fury, the hood moved his hand involuntarily toward his SMG, but Bolan had already hurried down to join a couple of guards lying behind the rampart of flat stones bordering the sunken garden.

Badmouthing J-P's number-one enforcer in front of his soldiers would have made Sondermann an enemy, for sure. Good, the Executioner thought. As yet he had no clear plan how he would approach the Mafia-KGB threat. But the more discord he could sow around here the better. If he was unable to conceal his dislike and contempt for carrion like Smiler it could at least provoke some kind of future action. And Bolan was a firm believer in mixing it and waiting to see what happened.

Right now it seemed that the battle for the island was damned near through. Most of the raiding party climbing up from the inlet had already been blown away by guards posted behind the house.

At least he need worry no longer about the body floating in the pool and the guy he had killed on the terrace: the attackers would be blamed for those.

He crouched near one of the guards sheltering behind the stones. The remainder of the invading force seemed to be holed up behind the summerhouse where he had first talked to Coralie Sanguinetti.

"How many d'you reckon?" he asked the man.

"Three or four," the hood replied. "Maybe a couple more inside the shack. Some of the boys are making it through the plantation—" he nodded toward a clump of trees on the seaward end of the isle "—and take 'em from the rear."

"We don't have to wait," Bolan said. He noticed a grenade hooked to the man's belt. "Mind if I borrow this?"

"Go ahead," the hood said. "But you'll never make it, guy. That cabin's more'n a hundred yards away. You can't throw that far on target."

"I don't figure on trying," Bolan said. "Give me covering fire, okay?"

He rose, holding the grenade in his right hand. Then, as the guard and his companions opened fire with a motley collection of shotguns and carbines, he dashed, bent double, through flower beds and rows of dwarf azaleas to dive headfirst into the pool.

He swam underwater to the far end, surfaced and pulled the pin from the grenade.

The gunners behind the summerhouse, who had opened up as soon as he began his run, were raking the patio with automatic fire.

Bolan braved the death hail and climbed the ladder. He flung the grenade with all his force over the shingled roof of the building, judging the throw accurately so that the deadly missile dropped among the raiders taking cover behind it.

The bomb exploded with a shattering roar, a vivid flash that momentarily lit the flowers and shrubs with an unnatural glare. There were no more gunshots.

The instant's silence that followed was broken by a man screaming. At the same time a heap of dead brushwood and garden refuse ignited by the explosion burst into flame behind the hut. Within seconds the flimsy wooden back wall was ablaze.

Flames shot skyward, fanned by the breeze. The rafters caught. Tiles fell and then the whole roof collapsed.

Two men ran out from the miniholocaust and were shot down at once by the guards. In the gory shambles behind the burning shack, one body still writhed.

"Bring him inside—and keep him alive until he's talked," Jean-Paul called from the terrace.

Lights came on all around the house. The gangsters' women, huddled together, could be seen anxiously peering through the windows. The capo from Marseilles stepped down into the garden and approached Bolan. "It seems we have to offer you a vote of thanks, guy," he said. "Like twice this same night."

"Part of the job." Bolan made his voice gruff. "That's what you're paying me for, isn't it?"

"Paying you...?" Jean-Paul stared at the wet-suited warrior, his brow knitted into a frown. Then suddenly the handsome face cleared. "Sondermann!" he exclaimed. "You're Kurt Sondermann, right?"

"When I'm not playing with fire!" Bolan said.

6

The man in the cellar was screaming again. Marcel Sanguinetti walked to the stereo and turned up the volume. He snapped his fingers at a white-coated waiter, ordering him to circulate more rapidly with his tray of champagne-filled glasses.

Conversation among the wives and mistresses of the gang bosses became shriller, boosting the pretense that they had heard nothing.

The wounded raider had cried out often enough as he was manhandled into the house from the gutted cabin. But that was because of the pain from the burns and injuries he had suffered in the bomb blast. Now the screams had a more desperate note. Smiler and his two buddies were in the cellar exercising their sinister skills on the nerves and flesh of an already ravaged body.

Bolan stood outside a huge salon. Scalese, Ancarani and the Toulon capo, Pasquale Lombardo, were standing by a window in a haze of cigar smoke. Borrone huddled with the three other Americans and the Parisian baron. Only Sanguinetti and the Sicilian, Arturo Zefarelli, were making any attempt to mix with the women.

The Executioner had declined to join the party on the excuse that a frogman suit was hardly ideal wear for a social occasion—even one that had been interrupted by an armed assault that he himself had been largely instrumental in repelling. His real reason was the fear of being recognized by the KGB colonel, Antonin.

Jean-Paul had introduced them when the attack was over, but Bolan had already pulled the helmet on again and the Russian had hardly glanced at him.

Bolan sipped a glass of champagne in the passageway between the salon and the bar. The waiter passed in and out with foaming bottles, hors d'oeuvres, fresh glasses.

Jean-Paul returned to the big room with Antonin in tow. Bolan figured they had been below to check out the information acquired by Smiler. "A few minutes more, Colonel," the gang boss had promised within Bolan's earshot.

Antonin nodded and turned to talk to a group of the younger women.

Jean-Paul moved among the guests, his thick white hair and tanned, handsome face conspicuous above the glare and glitter of the underdressed and overpainted females. The Executioner observed that Scalese, Ancarani and Lombardo stopped speaking as the capo from Marseilles approached them.

Bolan recalled that the Toulonnais boss had been the least enthusiastic of the hoods during the conference he had overheard, and the other two, besides throwing out the most challenging questions, had from time to time been whispering to each other.

Maybe their sudden silence now was due to fear. Or even politeness. But he filed the fact away in his mind for future reference.

Coralie Sanguinetti emerged from the kitchens and approached him. She was stuffing her small gun—it was a twenty-four ounce Semmerling LM-4 with a cobblestone Hogue combat grip—into her purse before she joined the party.

"It's a good professional lightweight," Bolan told her as she passed. "Looking at the guests, I reckon you'd be wiser keeping it handy."

She swung around and stared at him. "Herr Sondermann," she said coldly, "you may have assisted us in a material way, but please remember you are a guest in my father's house. If you don't like the company, you are quite free to leave."

Bolan was amused by the way this girl blew hot and cold. "Sorry to disappoint you, ma'am," he said, "but I'm afraid that's out of the question. I'm employed by one of your father's, uh, friends. I can't leave until I get his go-ahead."

She gave him a contemptuous look. "Is that why you are lurking in the servants' entrance?"

Before Bolan could think of a suitable reply, Jean-Paul himself came toward them. "My dear," he said, taking the girl's arm in a proprietorial way, "your father needs some help entertaining the guests."

"Whatever you say, darling," Coralie replied with a defiant glance at the Executioner. Tossing back her long hair, she strode into the salon.

Bolan shrugged. It was understandable that she would have been hostile, catching a stranger eavesdropping in her father's house. But she had seemed friendly and efficient during the firefight outside. But now the battle was won, suddenly he was bad news again.

No matter. He'd figure it out later. Jean-Paul interrupted his thoughts.

"You better come downstairs, Sondermann. Our bird is singing all right, but I want you to hear the last verse: you might need to learn some of the words.

They crossed the crowded room, threading their way among the guests. One or two of the hoods, and most of the women, stared curiously or appreciatively at the Executioner's tall, muscled, blacksuited physique. Antonin paused with his champagne glass halfway to his lips. This time, as he saw Bolan's blue eyes and the dark hair without the helmet, his brow creased in a frown. Then he turned away, and continued talking to Borrone.

Bolan was glad when they left the brightly lit room for the passageways honeycombing the extraordinary house.

Smiler met them at the door of the cellar. There was blood on his hands. "I'm sorry, boss," he apologized after a suspicious glance at the Executioner. "The bastard croaked on us. Maybe he was too far gone to start with."

Bolan looked beyond the hardman into a room with stone walls, part of which had been hollowed out of bedrock. The wounded attacker's end had not been pleasant.

"Reckon there was no more to tell, anyway," one of Smiler's henchmen told Jean-Paul. "We know who an' why an' how. Since you and the Russian left, we learned a little about this bastard's buddies and what they aim to do."

Bolan looked enquiringly at the gang leader. He was not supposed to know the background; it was reasonable that a new arrival should want to be filled in.

"We are about to start a new...project," J-P explained. "The details are not important. But I will tell you that certain hostile elements have been trying to wreck it. We thought we had eliminated them...but it seems we were mistaken. There are still some around."

"Would these be from the same stable as the gorillas who jumped me on the way down?" Bolan asked. He had given the Marseilles boss a full rundown on the gas-station ambush.

"Neighbors," J-P replied. "The soldiers you wasted there were Scotto's boys. These punks tonight were the tail end of a small time outfit run in Paris by a guy name of Secondini. Or so this loser said." He nodded toward the corpse.

"There's more, J-P," one of the hoods said.

"Such as?"

"There ain't no more Secondinis. But there's another team aiming to make it. They figure if you was outta the way and the plan with the Comrades fucked up, they could muscle in to your manor. Not worldwide...just your territory down here."

"Who?" Jean-Paul's voice was rock hard.

"The Corsicans. Balestre's old mob."

Jean-Paul slammed one fist into his other palm.

"Can't trust anyone, can you, boss?" Smiler said with a shake of his head. "I fixed that guy myself, personal. There wasn't even a piece of rope left after that buoy blew." His small, mean eyes flicked over Bolan as if he wished the Executioner and not the young Corsican had been his victim.

"What's their plan?" Jean-Paul said tightly. "Did he know? Did you get it out of him before he died?"

"Oh, sure." Smiler's mouth twitched in a grin that was pure evil. No prizes, Bolan thought, for guessing how he came by the name.

"Well?" The tanned face creased into an expression of impatience.

"They was in league with the Corsicans," Smiler said. "This lot, I mean. Balestre's boys were to be the backup detail—if the raid had worked out. They were waitin' for a signal."

"Where?"

"At sea. If they don't get the go-ahead by midnight, they play Cinderella and try again another day."

"You didn't find out the signal?"

Smiler shook his head. "This punk wasn't the boss. I don't think he knew."

"Does Ancarani know? About the whole deal, I mean."

"Not on your life," Smiler said. "Balestre and him, they weren't exactly buddies!"

Interesting, just the same, Bolan reflected: Jean-Paul was already unsure of the Corsican capo. He could use that later.

"The guys at sea, where do they run to? Balestre's hideout near Calvi?"

"I would think."

"This mess must be cleaned up," Jean-Paul said. "Fast. The Russian's already sore about tonight. We were supposed to have sewn up any possible opposition before he showed. Now he's staying for a couple of days instead of splitting tonight...and the slate has to be clean before he signs. So I guess it's a surprise party at Calvi tomorrow night."

He turned to Bolan. "You string along, Sondermann. We can use all the muscle we got. But first there's a couple of solo deals I want to talk to you about. We'll talk tomorrow."

He took Bolan's arm and piloted him away from the cellar.

"You got the retainer okay?" Jean-Paul asked as they climbed to the garden floor.

"Sure," Bolan lied. There had been very little money in the hit man's pockets or baggage. He guessed that whatever had been advanced to Sondermann would remain forever unclaimed in some discreet account in Hamburg or Switzerland.

"The terms are still agreeable to you?"

Bolan nodded.

"Good. You'd better get back then. I'll brief you tomorrow night. A car will call at your hotel. I'll have one of the guards run you back to Cassis in the launch."

"Forget it," Bolan said. "My car's just across the water. I'll take the rubber dinghy." He grinned. "I don't think the owners are going to need it again tonight."

Bolan left the dinghy at the foot of the bluff, dressed and drove back to the city. He found a pay phone on the old port, fed in coins, dialed eleven digits.

A girl's voice answered at once. "Yes?"

Bolan quoted an identification number and a password. The girl gave him a Paris number to call.

He memorized the number, waited half a minute and dialed it. The number, which was changed twice every day, was answered on the eighth ring. Bolan identified himself again, quoted the code number of the person he wished to speak to, waited while he was further checked and then patched in to a scrambler line.

"The ball game has started," he said when finally he was put through. "We have to meet and it's a red. Tomorrow, Number One on the list. No, make it midday. I expect to be killing some Corsicans in the evening!"

7

Mack Bolan took the early railcar east from Marseilles to the small shipbuilding port of La Ciotat. A sultry humidity had hazed the air and turned the sea from Mediterranean blue to a dull pewter color that merged with the sky.

Still, the long curving strip of shore that lined the bay beyond the old town was crowded. Oiled vacationers lay packed like sardines on the blistering sand. The water was busy with swimmers, windsurfers and pleasure boats. It seemed a far cry from the murderous exchanges less than twelve hours ago at La Rocaille.

Bolan intended it to be. Of the handful of passengers who had left the diesel railcar at the station, none, as far as he could see, had followed him to the beach. And he was sure no one had followed him when he boarded a bus bound for Bandol, farther along the coast. But there were such things as walkie-talkies and phones. He had already been tailed from Lyons to the gas station ambush and noticed nothing. And he still didn't know how many different teams might be gunning for him.

But today it was vital that none of the hoods, that nobody at all, knew of his rendezvous.

He left the bus at Bandol, dodged through a crowded fruit market and installed himself at a sidewalk café. There he ordered and paid for a drink, walked through to the men's room and left by a back entrance without returning to his table. After that he threaded his way around two floors of a department store and jumped another bus as the doors were closing.

The bus took him back to Aubagne, on the outskirts of Marseilles. From here he took a cab to Aix-en-Provence.

Telder was waiting for him in the fossil room of the city's natural-history museum. "Chamson's too well-known in these parts," the Swiss Interpol chief said. "We agreed that I should come alone."

"Good," Bolan said. "I'm pretty sure I wasn't tailed. But if I was, I think I lost him."

He glanced around. Bolan and Telder were the only visitors professing interest in the glass display cases.

"I'll give it to you straight," Bolan murmured. "There's a KGB plot to weld all the world's Mafia families into one supersyndicate of international crime, armed, funded, supplied—and probably directed eventually—by Moscow."

Telder pursed his lips in a soundless whistle. "To what end?"

"To undermine the power of all the Western police forces, of shooting and bombing and looting every country into a state of total anarchy. With the resulting chaos and panic...well, they figure the whole system will collapse, making way for a Red takeover."

"And the four murders we were investigating?"

"Gang bosses who didn't want to play ball. They were killed in a hurry to stop them from forming some kind of rival, non-KGB coalition."

Telder's eyes widened, but he remained silent. He was pretending to take notes from a caption inside one of the showcases. "What are the mafiosi supposed to get out of the partnership?" he finally asked.

"Money," Bolan said. "More than they ever dreamed of, even in their slime-bucket business. And I think they're dumb enough to believe they'll be allowed to exist, even to warrant special treatment, after the takeover!"

"Stupid asses," Telder said. "They'd get special treatment, all right. A private room in the Lubyanka. Can you imagine the comrades setting up a directorate for social-realist crime? Hell, they don't even admit they *have* any crime!"

"They've got crime," Bolan said soberly. "For export only. It's labeled KGB."

The Swiss smiled faintly. "Very well. What do we do about it?" he asked.

"There's nothing *you* can do about it," Bolan said. "You and Chamson, that is. No public crime's officially been committed...yet. There's only one line to take, and I'm the fall guy in the hot seat. It has to be done from the inside. And right now that's where I'm at."

"Done how?" Telder queried. "Killing all the family chiefs who are in on the deal? Even unofficially, I can't give a go-ahead on that."

Bolan shook his head. "They would be replaced, anyway. Same goes for the Russian masterminding the scheme. No, the only way is for the Mob as a whole to be unwilling to go through with it. That would choke off the KGB, make them see it's a no-go situation."

"But you said the Mafia already had agreed...?"

"Sure, for the moment. But to make it work, they have to be solid for this one-Mob, one-leader routine. Like the Nazis under Hitler. Without that, the KGB won't play. So the way I figure it, the Mob must be disunited."

"But how?" Telder asked again.

"Play one family against another. Arrange it so they're gunning for each other rather than the law. There were enough dissenters left to raid La Rocaille, even without leaders. It shouldn't be too difficult to play on existing rivalries and find a few more. It's been done before, back home. Working from the inside, I think I can do it here.''

"But it's got to be quick. The whole deal has to fall apart while Antonin's still down here.''

"You'll need help, then,'' Telder said. "What can we do?''

"There is something,'' Bolan said. "I have to keep my nose clean with my new boss. I already know of several contracts that Sondermann's been hired for. But I don't want to take out innocent guys just to keep my cover secure.''

The Swiss was still looking at him expectantly.

"They'll have to disappear all the same,'' Bolan said. "It has to look as if I really did zap them. But I can't fake gunning them down, maybe in front of witnesses. If I handed them over to your people, could you keep them under wraps, totally out of circulation, until the ball game's over?''

"It's strictly illegal, but...yes. We could even arrange news items reporting that the bodies had been found floating in the river, out at sea, whatever.''

"Great. That should keep my hardman image intact. And if the victims don't like being held incommunicado, you can tell them they're damned lucky not to be incommunicado forever.''

"I think you can leave the details to us,'' Telder said.

Bolan said, "As for the rest...well, I've made enemies already inside the organization. I can make more. Then it's just a question of pitting one group against the other.''

"We are aware of the risks you run,'' Telder said. "We are most...appreciative.'' His voice sank to a more conspiratorial note. "When you want us, you know the number to call." He nodded briefly, turned and walked out of the room.

Ten minutes later Bolan emerged from the museum and made his way toward the railroad station.

"Well, well. If it isn't the big man himself! And what are you doing in a dusty old museum in Aix?" a voice exclaimed just behind him.

Bolan swung around...and found himself face-to-face with Coralie Sanguinetti.

8

Bolan sat with the girl at a café table drinking *pastis*. Bright shafts of sunlight speared the shade beneath the broad leaves of the plane trees.

"I could ask you the same question," he said.

Bolan wondered if she had been ordered to shadow him.

"I'm studying philosophy," Coralie said. "Here at the university in Aix." She was friendly again now. Bolan didn't have the time to figure out why. "I'm not just a poor little rich girl, you know. I shall have to earn my own living sometime."

"Not taking over Daddy's business?"

"Do I look like that kind of person?"

"Frankly," Bolan said, "I'm not exactly sure what business your father is in. We're kind of sheltered up in northern Germany."

She flashed him a suspicious look. "He has the biggest machine-tool factory in Italy," she said. "He has controlling interest in a company that manufactures digital watches and calculators in Alsace. He imports computer hardware from Japan, and he's on the board of two major oil companies."

"But why would a guy that successful have friends like...like the people I work for?" Bolan queried.

"Let me ask you a question," Coralie said. "Why are you badmouthing people like Jean-Paul—a man with your reputation? I've heard about you, Herr Sondermann: you're what they call a hit man; you kill people—for money. They tell me you murdered nine already.''

"Only folks I didn't like," Bolan said gravely. He would dearly have liked to set the girl straight, but the words he wanted to say would come uneasily from the mouth of a Teutonic killer...and if he allowed himself to show her what he really felt about the mafiosi, his cover would be blown for good. He tried to change the subject.

"Do you know Jean-Paul well?" he asked.

"Since I was in diapers."

"I work for him, but I don't really know him yet. What is he like?"

"He's nice," Coralie said defensively. Bolan remembered the way the gang leader had taken her arm the night before. "He's got a better brain than most of the others. He's generous. And he's a caring man."

"But he hires a guy like me to come down all the way from Hamburg. For what?"

"Oh," she said with a pout, tossing back her hair. She drained her glass and set it carefully on the wrought-iron table. "When I first saw you in that gallery, before I knew who you were, I thought you might be... Oh, well. I guess one can misjudge people."

Bolan suddenly realized the truth behind her mood swings. He was not a vain man, but he was objectively aware that he was attractive to many women. Coralie Sanguinetti was trying—and failing so far—to relate a natural liking for him to her own instinctive distrust of anyone in Sondermann's line of business.

He felt sorry for the girl—sorrier still because she was also fighting another, harder, battle: loyalty to her father on one side, loathing for his associates on the other—but there was nothing he could do to help her. "Have another drink?" he asked.

She shook her head. "Thank you. I have a class at two o'clock."

Bolan watched her get up from the table. Many other eyes followed her as she walked to her car parked by the curb. A white Porsche 928—what else?

The Executioner frowned. He had a gut feeling that, given the right approach and the right conditions, he could make her into an ally. But right now he'd have to play it by ear. The one thing he knew was that any help she might offer in the future would not be to Kurt Sondermann....

For the moment, however, it was better that he reinforced that alter ego in her eyes. Back in character, he called out as she unlocked the door of the Porsche, "Don't do anything I wouldn't do!"

Coralie looked across the terrace at him as she slid behind the wheel. "Is there anything you wouldn't do?" she retorted.

9

The raid on the hideout used by gangsters from the Balestre mob was planned and carried out like a military operation, although there were no more than sixteen men involved. They were divided into two teams of three and a ten-man main force.

Jean-Paul had insisted that the attack be restricted to soldiers from his own Marseilles family. Ancarani, the Unione Corse boss from Ajaccio, had offered a large contingent from his own gang, but Jean-Paul had refused. Blood ties, cross-relationships and loyalties were so intermixed on the island, he pointed out, that the risk of a leak, warning Balestre's people, would be high if Corsicans were included. Ancarani was angry, but he had to admit it was true.

Another reason—unstated, but one that Mack Bolan privately shared—was the fact that Jean-Paul was not one hundred percent certain of Ancarani's reliability. Not because he was in sympathy with the Balestre mob, but because he seemed the least impressed of any of the capos by the idea of the KGB tie-up. And a refusal to go along with this had, after all, provoked the death of Balestre himself.

The assault was timed for midnight. Smiler and his two shadows had arrived at Bastia by air from Marseilles earlier in the evening. They were to make their way to the rendezvous in a rented car.

Jean-Paul, Bolan and a seven-foot ex-wrestler named Delacroix were making the trip by air, too...as jumpers, thanks to a bribed helicopter pilot who was supposed to be night-testing a new chopper slated for the Nice-Monaco shuttle. The others were coming by sea.

Corsica, lying eighty miles south of the Gulf of Genoa, is shaped like a fist, with the index finger pointing north at the mainland. The index, protected by five-hundred-foot cliffs, is the twenty-two-mile promontory of Cap Corse. Bastia is located at the base of that finger; Calvi—the nearest town to the Balestre hideout—is on the other side of the fist.

Between Calvi and the Cap stretches a treeless, uninhabited strip of granite known as the Desert of Agriates. It was here that the seaborne mafiosi were to land.

Inland from this bleak wilderness, Jean-Miguel Balestre had inherited several hundred acres of pasture that began on the far side of the Calvi-Bastia highway and rose toward the foothills of the mountains in the interior.

Bolan was told that the property was a sheep farm. Balestre had made his headquarters in a ranch-style frame house surrounded by dipping pens, a shearing barn and outbuildings. These were spacious enough to accommodate the few workers who tended the flock and the much larger number of villains who looked after his real business.

This had involved the smuggling of liquor, arms and stolen cigarette consignments from North Africa to France and Italy; the distribution of cocaine, heroin and hashish from the Middle East; and the supply to brothels in Ajaccio, Naples and Marseilles of young Arab girls bought in the slave markets of Somali and the Sudan.

Daringly, for there was an elite parachute regiment of the French Foreign Legion quartered in Calvi, the team had used desolate creeks on the deserted Agriates coast for the landing of this merchandise. Much of it was then forwarded to its ultimate destination by supposed tourists using commercial sea, land and air services, and in the false bottom of a high-speed diesel cruiser berthed at St. Florent, between the Agriates and Cap Corse.

For many months the operation had infuriated Ancarani and the other Unione Corse leaders based on Ajaccio, Bastia, Propriano and Bonifacio. If Balestre's murder had not been contracted because of his opposition to the KGB-Mafia alliance, it was likely, the Executioner had learned, that he would have been liquidated, anyway, because of the inroads his operation was making on their own business.

Balestre's team, working with him ever since he started on his own after the death of his father and a Camorra apprenticeship, were satisfied with the rackets they already controlled. And raking in more money would not compensate them for the loss of autonomy they would suffer as a small unit in a worldwide association.

"Bastards are smart, too," Jean-Paul told Bolan in the chopper. "Disciplined, crack shots and at least two good enough to lead if the boss is taken out. That pair will be your piece of the action."

"Where did Balestre get them?" Bolan asked.

"Young kids mostly. Trained them himself after he'd worked with the Camorra. Unemployment. Poor background. No prospects on the island."

And now, Bolan thought, even fewer prospects, because many of them soon would die. It bugged him like hell, that poverty notwithstanding, they lacked an ethic, a code for living that distinguished between good and bad.

But that was no view he could air in front of the underworld boss from the hottest town in France.

Bolan was wearing his combat blacksuit with the Beretta leathered beneath his left arm, two ammunition belts and half a dozen HE grenades clipped to the webbing of his chute harness. A Husqvarna 561 Express hunting rifle with an IR nightscope leaned against the empty seat beside him.

Jean-Paul, the white cap of hair hidden beneath a black knitted balaclava, was armed with an Uzi SMG and a French police-style Browning automatic. The ex-wrestler carried an Ingram MAC-10, but there was an African knobkerrie—a long-shaft nightstick with a weighted spherical head—looped to his belt. With his huge frame, abnormal height and a shaven, battler's skull, he looked formidable.

"You're the expert marksman, Sondermann." The gang leader returned to the subject as the chopper overflew the massive red granite fortress that dominated the huddled shingles of the old town and the pale crescent of Calvi's pleasure beach. "I want you to keep back and, like I say, pick off individual targets as I call them out. You'd be risking your life at close quarters if the boys storm the ranch house. We'll find you a good concealed position, not too far away. And only use the pistol if you're threatened, okay?"

"It's your money," Bolan said. "I'm only here to carry out orders."

The Frenchman shot him a sideways glance. "Just as long as that's understood," he said.

An enigmatic character, Bolan reflected. Their conversation so far had been restricted to banalities: confirmation of details already agreed upon with the real Sondermann through an intermediary; arrangements for where Bolan was to stay; when and where they met; how he was to be paid and what weapons he would need. Yet it was clear that the mafioso from Marseilles was a cut above the other mobsters in the south. He was cultured, intelligent rather than just smart, determined, ruthless...and lacking altogether the crudeness that characterized the others.

Bolan had not been consulted when the raid was planned. He was interested to see how it went. And how J-P reacted under fire.

The moon was already high in the cloudless sky. Bright light shone from the wrinkled surface of the sea.

The coastline slid away behind them as the chopper whined over citrus groves and the geometrical patterns of vineyards. For one of the few times in his life, Bolan was going into battle not giving a damn whether his side won or lost. He viewed the raid totally objectively: morally, each side was as bad as the other. Win or lose, his only concern was the chance that he might find some situation arising out of the operation that could be used to weaken the solidarity of the mobs who intended to combine under KGB rule.

A thin white ribbon of road curled among the patches of cultivation below them. Jean-Paul looked through the plexiglas at a mass of mountains to their right. He tapped the pilot on the shoulder. "Down to two thousand and we jump," he said.

Bolan rose from his seat and slung on the Husqvarna. There was no question of serial jumping after a hookup here: it was simply slide back the panel of the blister and go.

J-P was pointing to the moonlit countryside below. "The thick stand of trees enclosed by that big loop in the highway," he called over the helicopter's rotor whine. "The southern fringe, away from the road in ten minutes. Okay?"

Bolan nodded. He pulled the panel aside and jumped.

At that height it was necessary to pull the ripcord at once. Even then he was left little time to take in the landscape floating up with increasing speed to meet him. He was already well below the jagged crests of the mountains.

To his left the bleak expanse of the Desert of Agriates lay bone-white beneath the night sky. Somewhere among these granite outcrops was Jean-Paul's ten-man squad—who would have been offloaded from a trawler and landed in rubber dinghies two hours earlier. Somewhere down there those guys were humping heavy machine guns, Kalashnikovs, grenade launchers and certain other pieces of equipment over the stony ground toward the ranch.

Smiler and his men would already be in place. Bolan gazed upward. There was no sign of the other two canopies against the stars. The droning clatter of the chopper died away in the direction of Cap Corse and the ocean.

He maneuvered the shrouds, spilling air from the chute. The wood was rushing toward him. He could no longer see the highway. Beyond a slope of meadow, half-hidden among another grove of trees, the pale light gleamed on the roofs of what he guessed was the Balestre farm.

Bolan skimmed the upper branches of pines, flexed his knees and made a perfect landing fifty feet from the edge of the wood. He was an experienced jumper, remaining upright and rocksteady as the canopy bellied down behind him and collapsed in the long grass. One minute later his harness unclipped, the grenades transferred to the belt of his blacksuit, it was rolled up and hidden behind a bush under the trees.

He unslung the Husqvarna and waited. He neither heard nor saw the other two come down, but it seemed almost at once that his ears detected the low whistle, repeated three times, that he was waiting for. He replied—only once—and made his way toward the sound.

Delacroix and his leader were together two hundred yards nearer the ranch.

"Smiler, Raoul and Bertrand will have worked their way into the woods behind the ranch," Jean-Paul told Bolan in a low voice. "They'll hold their fire until the rats begin to leave the ship.

"Come again?"

"We want the Balestre gang—there may be between twenty and thirty of them in there—to think the frontal attack by the guys crossing the road from the desert, the detail advancing from the sea, is the only one. If they're getting the worst of it, they'll most likely run out the back and head for the interior."

"And into Smiler and his boys?"

"Right. If they figure they have a chance, they may fan out in front of the buildings and try a counterattack."

"And that's where we three start to operate?"

"You got it. In that case, they'd probably try some kind of encircling move from in back, as well."

Bolan nodded. "Toward Smiler. Okay. Seems simple and sensible. They won't have patrols out? Or dogs?"

"Uh-uh. They don't know that we know they aimed to be part of last night's scene. If the punk Smiler wasted was telling the truth, they'll all be in there working on a plan where they hit us."

"No electrified fences? Trip wires? Booby traps? No sensors or closed-circuit TV?" Bolan sounded surprised.

The Frenchman laughed. "Hell, no. You can do that kind of thing on a private island like La Rocaille. But this is right by a public highway. There *may* be sensors nearer the house, but we want them to know we're coming when we're that close, anyway!"

They were skirting the edge of the wood, the night breeze warm on their faces. Jean-Paul led the way through a gap in a stonewall, and suddenly the details of the ranch buildings were visible in the radiance of the moon.

The place lay at the top of a long slope of pastureland that was broken nearer the house by a complex of pens and sheep-dip troughs spread below the largest of the barns. A line of trees on the far side of the slope marked the course of the driveway that curled up from the road.

The gang leader stopped near a ramshackle shepherd's cabin with a tumbledown gap where the door had been and a gaping window that looked toward the ranch.

"You stay here," J-P said. "The range to the stoop is exactly 360 yards—we worked it out on a large-scale survey map. The average slope of the meadow is six degrees." He added further instructions, and then departed into the night with the silent ex-wrestler.

Bolan moved across to the glassless window and looked up at the house. Louvered shutters were closed all the way around the two stories. The moonlight was too bright to see if there were lights shining inside. It was very quiet in the abandoned hut.

The Husqvarna was propped against the rough stone wall. He picked up the rifle and hefted it experimentally. It was a beautifully crafted weapon—a .358 Magnum, with a two-foot blued steel barrel, a rosewood stock and a corrugated butt plate. It weighed, Bolan estimated, just under eight pounds.

He had chosen it because his briefing demanded a large-bore rifle, dead accurate at long ranges, with a heavy, high-velocity bullet and colossal stopping power. Some of the hoods had laughed at the gun because it was bolt-action with only a 3-shot magazine.

Bolan had retorted that it might be the slowest of all the repeaters for follow-up shots, but it was also the most reliable, since the marksman commanded the climb on each shot...and anyway, with the nightscope he had fitted, follow-up shots were rarely necessary!

The scope was a Balvar X5 by Bausch and Lomb. This, and a breech pressure of more than twenty tons p.s.i. and a superhigh muzzle velocity that gave the l50-grain slugs an almost flat trajectory, were enough to guarantee a gunner of Bolan's expertise better than an eighty percent chance of a first-time hit whenever the cross-hairs centered on a target.

He brushed dust and small fragments of stone and mortar from the flat sill of the window frame and leaned his elbows on it. With the butt pressed into his right shoulder, the big gun was heavy but beautifully balanced. Bolan wrapped his fingers around the pistol grip, hit a full magazine into the chamber, and flicked the bolt. The safety was already set in the firing position.

The scope's rubber eyeguard caressed his cheek and brow. Through the magnifying IR lens he could see the moonsplashed facade of the ranch-house. Testing the strength of the first-pressure prelim spring, he curled his right index around the trigger. The cross hairs were centered on the entrance doors.

In the distance a whistle shrilled.

It was echoed, louder, from closer at hand. Three piercing blasts. The seaborn detail had arrived; Jean-Paul had instructed them to go ahead.

Inside the house a dog barked. The sound was at once drowned by a staccato burst of automatic fire from the far side of the meadow. Bolan could see the muzzle-flashes winking in the shadow beneath the trees lining the driveway.

A shutter banged open and was slammed shut. Voices shouted inside the building. Glass shattered and fell, and a single ricochet screeched off the stone facing to the frame house.

The attackers unleashed another volley. It was repeated from the edge of the wood fifty yards to Bolan's left. And now there was an answering fire from the ranch. Flame stabbed the dark on the shadowed side of the building. Louvers were smashed aside, and guns sprouted from the shutters. Revolvers, automatic rifles and at least one SMG were aiming at the muzzle-flashes of the assault force.

Mack Bolan waited in the cool semidarkness of the shepherd's hut, watching the action.

The men from the sea were advancing up the driveway under cover of bushes that grew beneath the trees. The leading guns were within a hundred yards of the house now. Fire from the defenders redoubled: there were a lot of guys shooting from all windows on both floors, although automatic fire was shredding some of the wooden structures and making the position untenable. Bolan heard a high-pitched scream of agony, but whether it came from inside or outside he couldn't say.

Suddenly the seaborne detail's heavy machine gun opened up, the hard stammer of the belt-fed rounds punctuating the lighter crackle of machine pistols and SMGs. Beside it there was an abrupt glare, an express-train shriek and a streak of fire arrowing toward the ranch. Bolan knew the sound. Someone had fired a rocket grenade from a Russian RPG-7 launcher.

The shoulder-borne, bazooka style weapon fired a five-pound missile with directional fins that opened as soon as the grenade left the launch tube and the rocket booster ignited.

There was a thunderclap report as the deadly projectile hit the ranch-house stoop, burst on impact and ripped open the heavy double doors. Moments later a second grenade exploded in the hallway beyond. In the momentary flash of the detonation, Bolan saw masonry fall and splintered wood spin through the air, trailing spirals of smoke.

It was then that the attackers played their trump card. Somehow, from somewhere, Jean-Paul had acquired an ex-warplane 20 mm cannon and a single feed belt alternating high-explosive, armor-piercing and incendiary shells. Mounted on a modified tripod, the weapon roared to life, stitching the night with tracers that homed in on the gap blasted by the RPG-7.

The HE shells laid waste the front half of the house's lower floor. The armor-piercers, unsuited to this kind of assault, sheared through furniture, interior walls and anything else in their path until inertia and gravity overcame their speed and they dropped to burst somewhere in the back.

But the incendiaries did the real damage. A score of them, burning on impact for one-seventieth of a second at 2,000 degrees Celsius, screamed through the hole and ripped into the pine walls and wooden staircase at the rear of the hallway, setting them alight instantly.

Within seconds, flames, fanned by the draft sweeping in through the gap, were seething upward to set the floor of the upper story ablaze.

But the remnants of the Balestre gang were not without their own surprises. Indoors, men were yelling, but from one of the outbuildings at the side of the ranch an ancient four-wheel farm wagon loaded with bales of hay trundled into the moonlight. There were flames here, too, small ones that licked the tinder-dry bales...and spread...and increased...and then boiled skyward until the whole load had become a blazing torch.

A torch that was accurately directed down the slope, increasing speed as it hurtled with murderous aim at the place where the machine gun, the RPG-7 and the cannon were hidden; a torch that was piloted by the four hoods with SMGs who had started it rolling and were now racing behind it, sheltered by the flames and shooting as they ran.

Firing from the hip, they scored some hits among the attackers, but it was the blazing wagon that wreaked havoc.

Crashing into the undergrowth where the gun crews were hidden, it tipped over onto its side, spilling the burning fodder right and left. At once the sun-dried brushwood flared up; desiccated leaves on the lower branches of the trees caught fire; a ring of fire forty yards in diameter consumed the fringe of the wood and swelled outward across the grass of the pasture.

Ammunition buried beneath the flaming hay discharged like exploding firecrackers. A rocket grenade, ignited by the fierce heat, streaked a fiery trail into the sky and then self-destructed.

Once again Bolan savored the paradox of his situation, ready to fire but owing allegiance to neither side. If the Marseilles mob won, and he had helped them do it, this would obviously consolidate his position as Sondermann, the hit specialist, and prove his "loyalty" to J-P. If the defenders gained, on the other hand, it would surely widen the rift among the various Mafia factions and make the KGB tie-up less likely...which after all was the reason for Bolan's Sondermann masquerade in the first place.

From the branches of a tree behind the shack, Bolan heard the ripping-calico snarl of the gang boss's Uzi. Two of the gunmen stumbled and fell, jerking uncontrollably as their lifeblood soaked the moonlit grass.

And then the towering figure of Delacroix emerged from the fire, his singed hair smoking, tiny flames still traversing the shoulders of his flak jacket. Oblivious to the danger, the giant started swinging his knobkerrie, crushing the skull of one of the remaining hoods and dealing the last such a terrible blow on the temple that he dropped like a stone.

Delacroix beat out the flames with his bare hands and called in a hoarse voice, "Okay now, boss? Let 'em have it?" It was the first time Bolan had heard him speak.

"Go ahead," Jean-Paul's voice replied from the branches above.

The giant shouted an order. Immediately a dazzling beam of light sliced through the night from a spotlight located halfway along the driveway, illuminating every detail of the burning house.

The place was rapidly becoming an inferno. The whole upper floor was ablaze, and flames roared skyward beneath a pillar of black smoke that streamed out and up through the blasted porch.

Dark man shapes were running frantically right and left. Other figures were motionless on the stoop, one slumped head-downward over the sill of a shattered window.

"Sondermann!" Jean-Paul yelled. "Fat boy and the man in red! Coming out now!"

Staring through the nightscope, Bolan saw a group of defenders, firing what looked like Skorpion machine pistols, swarm through the charred doorway and fling themselves behind a stone balustrade that confined a terrace below the entrance steps.

They would be invisible to the attackers along the driveway and at the edge of the wood, Bolan figured, but from where he was he could see the heads and torsoes of several men.

Among them was a rugged type wearing a red nylon parka. Near him crouched a short, fat guy with massive shoulders and thick arms. The two of them seemed to have taken charge of the survivors: the man in red was waving his arms at men out of sight in the yard between the house and the shearing barn; Fat Boy was looking over his shoulder, shouting to someone in back of the house, where gunfire from Smiler and his companions now added to the pandemonium.

Bolan squinted again through the sight until the cross hairs settled between the shoulder blades of the guy in the parka. He held his breath.

Concentrated.

Squeezed the trigger.

The report of the big gun was deafening. His shoulder throbbed from the massive recoil. The bullet hurled the man in red across the terrace and tossed him like a rag-doll on the steps.

Bolan snicked the Husqvarna's bolt and swung the barrel slowly sideways until Fat Boy was in the center of the scope. The cross hairs sank until the junction was steadied above his shoulders on the column of his throat.

Bolan fired again. The 15-grain slug slammed into the guy's neck and almost tore his head from his body. He catapulted back against the stoop post and slid lifeless to the ground.

"Okay!" Jean-Paul shouted. "In for the kill now!"

Someone near the house fired a long burst from an SMG, and the searchlight faded to orange and died in an explosion of smashed glass. Now there were men running toward the house from all sides, zigzagging among the long pasture grass, firing as they came. Half a dozen spilled from the bushes lining the driveway; a couple more gave them covering fire; a survivor of the RPG-7 crew ran with Delacroix; Smiler and his companions raced around the corner of the barn. The sound of gunfire rose to a crescendo.

Jean-Paul dropped from his command post in the tree and followed. Bolan, obeying instructions, left the Husqvarna in the ruined cabin and brought up the rear. He unleathered the 93-R deathbringer, flipped off the safety catch and ran.

He was level with the sheep pens, dodging between the troughs when the hidden gunman fired.

He must have been lying low, waiting for the chance to bring someone down from behind. Bolan was less than ten yards away when the gunner triggered a 3-shot burst.

The Executioner owed his life to a tussock of coarse sheep grass, which tripped him the instant the killer fired.

He pitched forward as the triple report rang in his ears, momentarily deafening him. He felt the wind of the heavy slugs stir the hair on top of his head...and at the same time a searing pain across his left shoulder.

Bolan hit the ground, rolled over and lay still.

The Beretta, knocked from his grasp by the unexpectedness of the attack, had spun out of reach. If he moved, the hidden gunman could hardly miss a second time. He used the oldest trick in the trade: he played possum.

Lying on his back at an unnatural angle, the injured arm doubled beneath him, he allowed his jaw to drop, breathing as shallowly as possible and forcing his eyes to remain open. He hoped that any movement he made would be mistaken for a trick of the red light flickering from the burning house.

Ten seconds passed...twenty...half a minute.

Slowly a bulky silhouette rose into view from behind a fallen tree to one side of the pens. Cautiously, his gun close to the hip to minimize recoil, he advanced on Bolan's supine figure.

Bolan held his breath, hearing the shots and the shouting at the ranch as if from a great distance. He knew that he was very near death. If the gunman was not satisfied...

The man stood over him, staring down.

Would he fire a final shot, just to make sure?

Inserting a toe beneath the Executioner's waist, he began levering the body over onto its face. So it was to be the neck.

Pain streaked through Bolan as he moved, but he kept on rolling, fast, and the shot was deflected as he went for the guy's wrist. Stooping over a man he thought was dead or dying, the killer was off balance and unprepared, and it was not too difficult for Bolan to take him by surprise.

The hood was big and strong. But a man in fear of imminent death is desperate. Bolan worked on his attacker with the strength of a crazy man. Ignoring the pain in his shoulder, he hurled the two of them across five yards of rough earth and bent the mafiosi backward over one of the troughs.

The shallow wooden trench was still half full of the chemical-smelling dip. Bolan locked his good arm around the guy's neck and forced him around. Then the Executioner struggled with all his strength until the man's head was down and his face touched the disinfectant.

His head went under the surface of the tar water and a shrill bubbling sounded over the distant gunfire. His legs kicked convulsively and he scrabbled to bring up his gun arm, but Bolan felt for the thumb and bent it back until it snapped and the killer screamed under the liquid.

Bolan increased the pressure on the neck lock, freeing the hand on his wounded arm to feel for the weapon. The hardman's fingers were nerveless and Bolan pried them away, jerking the gun clear. It splashed into another trough behind them.

The hood bucked violently, kicking his legs and twisting his body so that he fell entirely into the trough.

The killer's arms flailed uselessly, his hands clawed for a purchase, his breath gargled in his tortured throat as the fluid in the trough foamed and splashed.

Bolan wrenched his neck again, remorselessly forcing his nose and mouth beneath the surface, holding the man there until the bubbling deathscream subsided and the body went limp.

He left the corpse in the trough and hurried, still panting, up to the house. The flames were dying; the fight was over.

Jean-Paul was sitting on the steps. He looked up as the Executioner approached. "Good shooting," he said. "Once those two were down it was just a matter of time."

Bolan grinned. It was the first time since Vietnam that he had fought a battle under another's orders...and the first battle in which he had fired only three shots.

"How many did we lose?" Bolan asked Jean-Paul.

"Three under that blazing hay wagon. Two when we rushed the house. One on the driveway. And there's two wounded, one badly."

"So counting those two, if Smiler junks the car, that still leaves ten to make it across the Agriates, take the dinghies and get back to the trawler?"

"That's right," the gang boss agreed cheerfully. "It all works out fine in the end, you see."

"There's one more question," Bolan said, rising to his feet. "You said this was a sheep farm. Where are the sheep? And the shepherds?"

Jean-Paul laughed. "Summer pastures. They take them up into the mountains for three months while the weather's hot. I wouldn't want to run the risk of this kind of operation if there were animals around that could get hurt."

10

"Perhaps now," Jean-Paul said to Bolan the following afternoon, "we can go ahead with the amalgamation I was telling you about. There are a few details for you to take care of, and then it should be plain sailing all the way."

They were sitting in the enormous sun lounge of the mobster's house, which was cantilevered out from the cliffs to the east of Marseilles. A high stone wall surrounded the property, and closed-circuit TV monitored the electrically operated gates, but otherwise there seemed to be no special protection for the acre and a half of rare shrubs and exotic flowers landscaped around the steel-and-glass building. A white Mercedes convertible stood outside the closed doors of a three-car garage.

"What details did you have in mind?" Bolan asked.

"Four contracts," Jean-Paul said. He had given Bolan a brief rundown on the KGB project and the difficulties they had encountered. "Four guys who could still louse up the deal by shooting off their mouths in the wrong place."

"Who?"

"A lawyer, a newspaper columnist, a cop and a local television personality who's obligated to me and wants off the hook."

"You want to give me the details now?"

"Okay. Sooner the better. But what about your shoulder?"

"No problem," Bolan said. "It was hardly even a flesh wound. It'll be okay tomorrow. In any case, the Husqvarna kicks the other shoulder!"

There was a look of admiration in Jean-Paul's eyes as he watched the hired hit man.

"The lawyer's name is Maître Delpêche. Too damned smart for his own good. He made the mistake of advising an adverse party while he was representing me, at the same time, on the same case."

"He lives here in Marseilles?" Bolan asked.

"Oh, sure. The TV guy's name is Michel Lasalle. But he works out of the local Number 3 channel studios down here. You'll have no trouble locating him; he loves to be seen in public. You probably heard of the columnist. Georges Dassin. He's syndicated, likes to run after high-school girls—pays them to pose for nude photos! Trouble is, he was once a foreign correspondent in Moscow and he knows Antonin. If he sees the Russian here—and the guy has his sources—he might just put two and two together and run some damn fool piece trying to stir the cops on our payroll into action, and that could be embarrassing."

"Who's my cop?" Bolan asked. "A guy who's *not* on the payroll?"

Before Jean-Paul could answer, the sound of a diesel engine in low gear penetrated the glass. J-P stood and crossed to the window. "It's a cab," he said. "Looks like Antonin himself sitting in back. What the hell does he want this time of day?"

Bolan cursed under his breath. The last thing he needed was a confrontation with the Russian. The guy had been dubious, something stirring in his memory, the second time he'd seen the Executioner at La Rocaille. This time, wearing no wet suit, Bolan was certain he would be recognized.

"Maybe I'd better go," he said hastily. "You'll have business to discuss…and, anyway, there are a couple of calls I have to make—" he glanced at his Rolex "—before five."

"You can phone from here," the mobster said. "Besides, I'd like you in on this if he's going to talk about—"

"I don't have the numbers here. And they're unlisted," Bolan improvised. "You want quick service on these contracts, I have to get back to my hotel, check out those numbers, and—"

"Darling?"

The two men swung around. Jean-Paul's pretty dark wife, Séverine, was standing in the doorway. "J-P, darling, may I borrow Herr Sondermann for two minutes? Coralie's with me and she's got a problem with a passage of Hegel she has to translate for one of her test papers. If Herr Sondermann wouldn't mind…?"

"Of course, I'd be glad to help," Bolan said quickly. He looked enquiringly at the gang boss.

"Oh…very well." Jean-Paul shrugged. He found it hard to refuse his young wife. "Don't keep him long."

Walking through the black-and-white checkerboard marble hallway, Bolan saw through the armored glass entrance doors that the Russian was getting out of his cab.

But he wasn't paying the driver; he was asking him to wait. Bolan hoped the quote from Hegel was a long one.

Following Séverine along a corridor that led to the back of the house, Bolan passed Raoul, one of Smiler's lieutenants, in a white linen butler's jacket, on his way to answer the doorbell.

Coralie was in a den, sitting at a table strewn with textbooks and papers. "Surprise," Bolan said. "What seems to be the linguistic trouble?"

"As you're being paid, anyway," the girl said dismissively, "I didn't see why you shouldn't do some work for me."

"Coralie!" Sévérine sounded shocked.

"It's okay," Bolan said, smiling. "Mademoiselle Sanguinetti and I are old adversaries!"

In fact there were very few translation difficulties in the Hegel passage, but Coralie managed to keep the questions coming until they heard the distant slam of a car door, and Antonin's taxi drove away.

She accompanied him back to the sun room to apologize to J-P for the length of time she had kept him.

"Why did you do it?" Bolan whispered as they crossed the hallway. "That was a put-up job, wasn't it? You had Sévérine come in and ask for me deliberately, to keep me out of the way of the Russian? Thanks—but why?"

She glanced at him from the corner of her eye. "I think they call it woman's intuition," she said demurely. "I saw your face when you had to pass near him the night of my father's...party. I figured anyone who looked that apprehensive must be in need of care and protection."

Before Bolan could think of a suitable reply, they were back in the sun room.

"It was of no importance," J-P told Bolan when the girl had made her excuses and left. "Antonin's going to be away a couple of days, that's all. He wanted me to know: he's been recalled for consultations."

"To Moscow?"

"Hell, no. To his base. They fly him here in a chopper from one of those so-called Soviet factory ships—they're electronic surveillance vessels really—outside the twelve-mile limit."

"You were going to tell me," Bolan said, "about the contract for your cop."

"Oh, yeah," Jean-Paul said. "The cop. His face has been seen around here too much recently. A wise guy, asking questions. I figure he's dangerous to the project, so he must go. You can waste the others any way you want, but this one I want shot down in public. As a warning to others."

"What's his name?" Bolan asked. He could see the muscles in Jean-Paul's jaw working before he almost spat the word.

"Telder."

11

The phone calls that Bolan made were urgent. Antonin would be back in a couple of days. He would expect to find the mafiosi ready to sign on the dotted line. With all their internal problems settled. Which meant that Jean-Paul would expect his highly-paid German hit man to have wrapped up his first four contracts.

The Executioner had no wish to massacre four innocent men, but to contrive the satisfactory "death"—or at least disappearance—of the columnist, the lawyer and the TV personality, with or without their cooperation, depending on how scared he could make them, would be difficult enough in two days.

The "murder" of Telder would be something else.

"There's a convention of cops and criminologists and special services meeting in Avignon," Jean-Paul had told Bolan. "It ends tomorrow. Your man Telder is one of the guys on the platform. I'd like you to take him out during the windup session."

Bolan knew about the convention. The last call he'd made had been patched in to a secret number in the city. Ironically, the experts had been called together to discuss more effective measures against terrorism, skyjacking, juvenile delinquence and the increase in organized crime. "I want to make a point," J-P said. "Go chase the Arabs, the Armenians, the Libyans and all the other bomb-happy crackshots, but leave us alone. Do that and we leave you alone: otherwise...well, see what happens.''

"You want this guy Telder wasted as an example of what we could do?'' Bolan asked.

"Right.''

"But...in the conference hall itself? While they're all there?''

The gang leader nodded.

"How many at the convention?''

"Around two hundred. Security's tight, of course. But we can get you an official pass. And we have friends inside.''

"You're kidding,'' Bolan said. "This is a 561 Express that I use. Hell, the barrel's two feet long! I can't hobble in there with the gun stuffed down my pant leg, pretending I got too close to a bomb in Beirut!''

"So?''

"So I have to find some way of zapping the guy inside while I'm on the outside. If it has to be while he's on the platform.''

"It does. That's the way I want it. But I don't see why you have to use the rifle. Why not go in close and use a handgun? We can get you in there, gun and all.''

"It's getting out that has me worried,'' Bolan said. "I don't want to be lynched by a couple of hundred mad cop lovers. And that's what would happen if I tried anything from that close.''

"I don't see how it could be done from outside.''

"Let's go see the place,'' Bolan said. "If I'm the trig-german, I decide where; you just decide when. Okay?''

Jean-Paul shrugged. He glared at the hired gun. God-damn nerve. "I'll drive you there,'' he said curtly.

They went in the white Mercedes convertible. Like a spoiled child refused a second ice-cream, J-P ventilated his ill temper via the car. They covered the sixty-odd miles of expressway between Marseilles and the Avignon turnoff in twenty-nine minutes, hitting an average of just over 120 mph. And that included two stops demanded by highway patrolmen who handed out speeding tickets. Bolan was amused.

The convention was being held in the lecture hall of a modern high school, which was closed for the summer vacation. The hall was a large free-standing rectangle with a serrated, asymmetrically pitch roof like a factory workshop. The shorter, near-vertical slope of each serration was glass, to capture the north light and minimize the glare of the sun.

Behind the hall were the school buildings; in front there was a parking lot—glittering now with ranks of expensive cars—and the main gates that opened off a traffic circle fed by five broad avenues.

Bolan was interested in a narrow side street that led off one of the avenues, north of the school and less than one hundred yards from the intersection. The street was fronted by tall nineteenth-century houses with gray slate roofs and iron balconies on each of the six floors. Each building was ranged around a central courtyard with an archway that led to the street. Between the archways, small shops shaded their display windows against the sun.

Bolan walked through to the cobblestone yard behind the third archway and looked up at the apartments stacked on each side. The facade opposite the arch had been modernized: wide picture windows, flower-strewn concrete terraces, a flat roof. "Who owns that part of the building?" he asked.

"Friends of mine, as it happens," J-P said.

"And this side, backing onto the street?"

"Friends of friends."

"Great. Is there anyone in either of those two blocks that you or your friends could lean on a little? Anyone you have a lever on? I don't mean for muscle; just a helping hand for a few minutes."

"Listen, Sondermann," said J-P, "there isn't anyone in this town, or my town, that I can't get some kind of a lever on."

"Better still."

"What do you have in mind?" the gang boss asked curiously.

Bolan told him.

"You must be mad!" Jean-Paul said. "It must be at least three hundred yards."

"Of course it has to be the right time, with the right light, but given the help I'm asking for, it's a piece of cake."

"But the angle...the deflection...you'd never make it."

"I'll earn my money," Bolan said.

MAÎTRE DELPÊCHE was the difficult one. He could not accept the fact that someone wanted him dead.

Dassin, the columnist who cherished a secret passion for high-school girls, thought it was a joke. "What is this?" he said good-humoredly when Bolan showed him the Beretta.

"Look, Dassin," Bolan snapped. "I've been hired to kill you. But for reasons of my own, I don't want to do this one...but for other reasons, equally vital, it's got to look as if the contract's been filled."

"No way!" the newspaperman chided.

Bolan pulled back the slide on the auto-loader.

"All I have to do is fire a single shot into your temple and put the gun into your hand before I push you out the window. There'll be a suicide note, too. Something about underage kids and photos."

"You're serious, aren't you?" Dassin's voice was suddenly shaky.

"Damn right," Bolan growled.

"I'll come with you," Dassin said.

Bolan took a bleeper from his pocket, thumbed a button and spoke a single word. It was necessary to have witnesses who could support the theory of an abduction, so Bolan walked behind the columnist, a folded topcoat over one arm, as they walked out through the Provençal's entrance lobby. There was no reason for Dassin to put on an act: he looked scared enough to convince anyone that the tall, dark stranger with the ice-chip eyes held a gun on him.

A block away, the two men got into a black Peugeot sedan with tinted windows. Bolan was dropped off a mile farther on. Dassin and the three other men in the car drove north to a safe house built into a ruined castle.

Bolan was waiting in the underground garage of Michel Lasalle's plush apartment block. The TV broadcaster's handsome face paled the moment he stepped out of his Alfa Romeo and saw the dim shape of the Executioner, half-hidden in the shadow cast by a concrete pillar at one side of his parking slot.

Bolan had no trouble persuading the young man to step into the nondescript van standing nearby with its engine idling. Lasalle's hands were shaking as he sank into the passenger seat.

The takeover—in a black Citroën this time—was in a rest area on the Marseilles-Aix expressway. Lasalle would be kept isolated in a motel near Toulon until Bolan gave the word.

Fortunately for Bolan, Maître Delpêche was working late in his office near the cathedral. But the Executioner's luck ended there. Delpêche was a courtroom bully who gained most of his acquittals—especially in the defense of criminals—by intimidating witnesses. His work had given him an angle on the underworld.

"Who the *hell* do you think you are?" he stormed when Bolan, easing himself, gun in hand, through the half-open door, had said his piece. "What kind of hoax is this?"

"No hoax. There's a contract—" Bolan began.

"Bullshit! There's not a villain in the country who'd want *me* out of the way; there isn't one who'd dare. If it wasn't for me, most of the bastards would be in jail, anyway."

Bolan folded down the Beretta's front handgrip.

Delpêche was sitting in a swivel chair behind his desk. He swung left and right, shaking his head. "I don't believe you have orders to kill anyone. This is some kind of amateur attempt at a shakedown, isn't it?"

Bolan approached the desk. "I kill you...or we make it *look* as if I killed you. I get paid either way, as long as you stay out of sight until I leave town."

"So kill me," the lawyer said.

Bolan hesitated.

"No?" the lawyer said. "I thought not. And I'm going to call the police." He reached for the telephone.

The Executioner frowned. The last thing he needed was a confrontation with the local law. And the cop or cops in question just might be on Jean-Paul's payroll...and if he discovered that Bolan was trying to fake the hits he had been hired to make, the whole scheme—and Bolan's cover with it—would be blown wide open.

Delpêche was dialing.

"Central Commissariat? Delpêche speaking. Look, I want to report an attempt—"

Bolan crashed the barrel of the Beretta down on the receiver rest, cutting off communication. Delpêche looked up, a cynical smile twisting his features. "Just as I thought..." he began.

Bolan's left fist traveled only a short distance, but it had all his weight—and all his exasperation—behind it. The blow caught Delpêche on the side of the jaw and knocked him cold.

Bolan picked up the unconscious lawyer, slung him over his shoulders and carried him to the service elevator.

He met nothing in the way of true resistance as they descended to the basement parking lot. Nobody saw him dump Delpêche's limp figure in the passenger seat of the lawyer's Jaguar. But there was a barrier pole barring the exit at the foot of the ramp leading to the street. A uniformed guard in a glassed-in hut at one side of the pole was sharing a bottle of beer with the janitor.

Recognizing the car, he moved toward the lever that raised the barrier...and then, seeing Bolan at the wheel and the inert figure slumped beside him, he leaped for the doorway of the cabin, reaching for the revolver holstered at his waist.

Bolan was out of the car before the guy had time to draw his weapon. The Executioner fired two shots from the Beretta—deliberately high, above the heads of the two men, shattering the glass, wrecking an electric clock on the cabin wall.

"On the floor," he snapped. "Both of you, if you want to stay alive. Facedown. Hands above your heads."

The two men complied and Bolan plucked the guard's gun from its holster and sent it skittering away beneath the parked cars. While the two men quaked on the floor, he yanked the lever operating the barrier and ran back to the Jaguar. The big rear tires laid rubber on the ramp as he took off.

The warrior was satisfied how everything had worked out so far. The interrupted call to the police, added to the assault on the guard and his friend, who would have seen the lawyer's unconscious body in the car, would strengthen the abduction scenario. Bolan spoke into his transceiver.

Chamson and Telder's undercover operatives took Delpêche ten miles outside the city limits. "Keep a close watch on this one," Bolan advised. "He's tricky. Doesn't believe a thing he's told. If he still doubts the story when you guys fill him in...well, I guess that's just his bad luck!"

The Jaguar was abandoned near an unused gravel pit filled with stagnant water. Police frogmen would be dragging it for Delpêche's body within twenty-four hours.

There was blood, Delpêche's, on the Jaguar's beige leather seats. The lawyer's nose had been bleeding when Bolan put him in the car.

Beneath the seats, the investigators would find three more spent shells—Bolan had fired a burst into the air— that matched the two outside the cabin in the basement parking lot.

If that didn't add up to a prima facie case of kidnapping and murder, Bolan reflected grimly, nothing would.

12

Bolan was wearing a white coverall when he approached the police line with Raoul, the stockier of Smiler's henchmen.

Raoul was similarly dressed. He was carrying a canvas case and there was a short aluminum ladder supported on his left shoulder. Bolan's hands were weighed down with two five-kilo cans of anticorrosion paint that had already been opened and partly used. Paintbrush handles projected from the knee pocket of his coverall.

The avenues were not lined with police the way they would have been if the convention had involved visiting diplomats or French senators. But three gray armored trucks, used to carry anti-riot squads, were parked off the traffic circle, and there were police details on each sidewalk of all five approach roads. Gendarmes with slung SMGs guarded the entrance to the school complex. More men patrolled inside.

Bolan and the mobster were stopped before they reached the side street. "Where are you going?" one of the cops asked.

"Number three," Bolan said, jerking his head toward the street. "The guttering above the arch is rotted; the tenants complained that it leaks. So the landlord finally decided to have it fixed."

"Your papers?"

They produced them—dog-eared folders that identified them as workmen employed by a local contractor; in Bolan's case a residence permit, also, stating that he was an immigrant of German origin. Jean-Paul was good at that kind of detail.

"What's in that case?" another cop demanded.

Raoul unzipped the canvas bag. Inside were more paint brushes, a can of thinner, cotton waste, a coil of rope, a plastic bottle of cheap red wine and two ham sandwiches wrapped in cellophane.

The first cop handed back the papers. "Go ahead," he said.

Bolan glanced across at the armored vehicles. "What's going on?" he asked.

"Just routine. A stack of bigwigs meeting in the school over there."

"Some people have all the luck," Bolan said. "We never got police protection when *I* went to school!"

The cops laughed and waved them on.

They walked unhurriedly to the third house in the street. On the inner side of the arch they found a painter's scaffold that had been suspended from booms projecting from the roofline above. They stepped into the wooden lift and Bolan checked the hook, shackle and swivel assemblies on the end of each hoisting cable. When he was satisfied he nodded and they began to haul on the ropes that ran over pulleys on the outer ends of the booms. The cradle jerked upward, accompanied by the squeak of the pulley wheels as they revolved.

Braking the cradle below the guttering, they began slapping the anticorrosion paint on a section that stretched from the arch to the corner of the yard.

It was almost midday. White continents of cumulus cloud moved slowly across the blue sky, hiding the sun from time to time. But right now it was hot as hell, and the steep roofs above shut them off from the breeze. Soon Bolan and his companion were dripping with sweat.

"Shit," Raoul complained, leaving his brush dipped in the paint can and massaging his right arm. "My goddamn shoulder is aching. Why the hell do we have to waste time horsing around in this elevator, anyway?"

"You know why," Bolan said. "The cover has to be perfect."

"I don't see why we need two guys. You could handle the whole deal. I can't help you press the goddamn trigger, after all."

"Painters work with a mate," Bolan said. "Anyway, that's the way J-P wanted it. He figured I'd need a good backup man."

In truth it was Bolan himself who had insisted that someone the gang boss trusted should come with him. Raoul's report of what he had seen Bolan do was vital.

The mobster was not soothed by the implied compliment. He spit over the side of the cradle. "It beats me," he grumbled. "I coulda been helpin' Smiler work over that creep who owns the café in the Old Port. The asshole won't come across with his insurance payment.

"You like that kind of work, don't you?" Bolan asked, concealing his revulsion.

"Sure. I'd rather be in the contract line, though. Like with Smiler the other day..." An ugly smile cracked open the hood's blue-jowled jaw. "I'll never forget the look on Frankie Secondini's face when we told him! We were on this train, see, and I had this length of steel—"

"Yeah," Bolan said curtly. "I heard."

At midday the sun disappeared behind a cloud and a factory whistle sounded in the distance. The convention

was due to remain in session for another hour, breaking for
lunch at one o'clock.

"Okay," Bolan said. "We're on our way."

He drew on rubber gloves and fished plastic-wrapped
packages from beneath the paint in each can. Inside one
was a small but powerful pair of Zeiss binoculars which he
handed to Raoul. The other contained a dayview Balvar
X5 sniperscope, similar to the one Bolan had used in Corsica but without the Triphium Ir light source. He placed
this in his knee pocket and extended the ladder so that it
linked the cradle with the roof.

Followed by Raoul, he climbed to the roof. They were
wearing rubber-soled sneakers. Carefully, crouching just
below the line of the roof, they circled the block above the
courtyard until they came to the modernized sector opposite the archway. From here they looked over a row of
lower buildings to the nearest avenue and the school beyond. The sidewalks were crowded now with office workers and clerks from the stores hurrying to lunch.

In the center of the flat roof a rectangular structure eight
feet square and ten feet high housed the mechanism at the
top of an elevator shaft. Between this and the roof parapet on the side away from the courtyard half a dozen zinc
ventilator outlets from the air-conditioning plant projected. Bolan consulted his watch. "Three minutes," he
said.

Raoul sank gratefully with his back against the elevator
housing. The sun was shining again, and the tarmac surface of the roof was softening in the heat.

Bolan stared over the buildings below them to the far
side of the avenue, where the near-vertical slopes of the
assembly-hall glinted in the bright light.

He looked at the sky. Another bank of clouds was drifting across from the west. Soon the sun would be hidden once more.

Two minutes later he walked to the ventilator nearest the elevator housing. Seizing the conical cap that shielded the opening at the top of the twelve-inch metal tube, he twisted left and right until the cone and its stays loosened.

He lifted off the cap, glanced again at his watch and held his hand out to Raoul. The hood handed him the coil of rope.

One end of it was spliced around an oval eyelet lined with lead. Using this as a sinker, Bolan fed the rope slowly into the ventilation shaft, playing it out until he felt it slacken in his hands and there was a definite tug from far below.

The janitor—one of the people on whom Jean-Paul could use a "lever"—had been instructed to wait at the foot of the shaft at precisely twelve-fifteen.

Bolan waited until he felt three tugs on the rope and then began hauling it up again. It was much heavier this time. Carefully and evenly he withdrew the rope until the object tied to it appeared at the top of the vent.

The Executioner held the Husqvarna 561 in his hands.

He untied the rope and left it coiled by the shaft, then took the scope from his pocket and fitted it to the gun. Crouching low now, he moved to the corner where the parapet ran into deep shadow cast by a multiple stack of chimneys above the next-door building.

Kneeling behind the parapet, he rested his elbows on the coping and raised the butt of the rifle to his shoulder.

The school was due south of them, and the sun was almost directly above the assembly hall's serrated roof. The north-facing glass, four floors below Bolan's vantage point, was in shadow, but the glare from the sky allowed him to see through.

Bolan waited until the fringe of the approaching cloud bank passed across the sun.

At once, through the scope's magnifying lens, he was able to see through and into the hall.

He saw a quarter of a circle of tiered seats crammed with people around and above a high platform at the far end of the huge room. On the platform, eight men and a woman sat behind a long table, each with a microphone positioned nearby.

Three places away from the chairman sat Telder. He was busy scribbling on a pad in front of him. Some refraction in the roof glass was making it hard to define his outline. Bolan moved along the balustrade until he could sight the platform through a different panel in the roof.

The image was sharp and clear now. He took a 3-round clip from his breast pocket and handed it to Raoul. The mobster fed three 150-grain slugs into it and passed it back to Bolan.

The Executioner shifted his position slightly, until he was comfortable and totally relaxed. He maneuvered the Husqvarna until the Bausch and Lomb scope located the platform...the table..the nine experts...Telder.

The cross hairs centered experimentally on the Interpol man's chest.

The cloud thinned, became translucent. The sun rode out through thin veils of white into a clear blue sky.

The image blurred and vanished. At once it was uncomfortably hot again. Even in the shadowed corner of the flat roof, Bolan sensed the heat beating through his coverall. Sweat ran into his eyes from beneath his hair, crawled along his spine and trickled down his sides. His palms were sticky and his fingertips moist.

Bolan smothered a curse. He rubbed his sleeve across his brow; he wiped the palm of his trigger hand on the coverall pants. He stole a covert glance at his watch. Telder was due to address the convention; he was the last speaker before lunch.

The glass of the eyepiece was filmed with moisture. It was in any case impossible to see through the assembly-hall roof until the glare from the sun diminished.

Bolan looked yet again at the sky. Another mass of cumulus was moving toward the sun, but it would be several minutes before the glare was gone.

Raoul was squinting through his binoculars. "Last thing I saw, your mark was on his feet and talkin'," he said.

Bolan reached into the grip for a clean cotton cloth and wiped the eyepiece. He mopped his brow, keeping the sweat away from his eyes. He dried his hands for the second time.

Abruptly the heat was withdrawn as the tower of cumulus leaned forward and covered the sun. Bolan clicked the Husqvarna magazine in place and took up his position afresh.

Through the glass now he could see Telder on his feet behind the table, his notes in his hand. The first shot was to break the roof glass; that was essential—to alert the audience that something was happening, to convince Raoul, and to make a clear passage for the second and third.

He squeezed the trigger.

The thunderous report...the shock of the recoil...an impression through the magnifying lens of pandemonium: glass fragments in a frozen cascade, open mouths, men and women starting to their feet, staring upward, the chairman half-risen from his chair. Telder had halted in midphrase, his arms spread wide, an arrested gesture.

Bolan flipped the Husqvarna's bolt. The cross hairs lowered, shifted sideways, centered on Telder's chest. While he remained immobile, perhaps petrified with astonishment, Bolan held his breath, took up the first pressure, squeezed again.

The second coughing explosion. A click of the bolt, the glint of a cartridge case, slam the last round in and at once—*now!*—fire for the third time.

They both saw it—Raoul via the Zeiss prisms, Bolan through the Balvar scope. Telder fell to the back of the platform, his chair flung aside, a scarlet patch already blooming horribly across the front of his pale jacket. He hit the wall and slid to the floor.

Raoul was giggling. Bolan scooped up the three ejected shell cases and tossed them onto the roofs below. Seconds later he was lashing the rope around the rifle, complete this time with sniperscope and empty magazine, using the leather strap to tie on the binoculars. He lowered the gun into the shaft and began playing out the rope.

When three sharp tugs told him that the janitor had safely received the rifle, he let go the remainder of the coil and allowed it to snake down the tube.

While Raoul, still grinning with obscene glee, grabbed the canvas case, Bolan replaced the ventilator cone. By the time the police began any house-to-house search for the assassin, the Husqvarna would be back in its rack in the gun shop from which Jean-Paul had taken it.

In the distance, police whistles shrilled. Soon afterward, Bolan heard the crescendo warble of approaching patrol cars and the siren of an ambulance racing to the assembly hall. He hurried back toward the roof and the ladder.

By the time armored-truck details appeared in the courtyard below, Bolan and the mobster were sitting in the painter's cradle, eating their sandwiches and sharing the wine from the plastic bottle.

13

For Mack Bolan it was one hell of a situation. Correction: two separate hells.

For starters, Bolan was fighting, or pretending to fight, on the side of the savages. And second, instead of riding the crest of that usual one-man wave, the warrior's own plan forced him to lie low, working in the dark, using the plotters' own underhand techniques in order to force them to destroy each other.

It was the only way that he could be sure to provoke a rift in the planned association that would rupture any chance of a worldwide Mafia league and disenchant the KGB's Colonel Antonin sufficiently to make him throw the whole idea out the window.

This time the frontal assault, the elimination of enemy key men that Bolan favored, would be useless: there would always be others to take their places. No, the Soviet conspirators had to see the Mafia fighting family against family; they must be made to see the alliance as totally unstable...and therefore unreliable. Only then would they withdraw their support.

And, yeah, the Executioner was the only man who could do it.

From his position of trust he had to engineer a series of deceits and apparent treacheries that would split the syndicate apart like an overripe melon.

Okay, that position was now well established. After the disappearance of three men and the public murder of a fourth, Bolan in his role of the German hit man was well in with the high command of the Riviera Mafia.

But it was only now that the really hard part began.

And there were dangers.

The ever-present threat of a confrontation with Antonin.

The fact that now, as an accepted man in the organization, Bolan would be expected to take part in group operations, in crimes that would be difficult to avoid without blowing his cover or faking them as he had done with Telder.

The Telder operation had been impressive: it was Raoul's reluctantly admiring report, and the newspaper accounts of this and the other three disappearances, that had finally raised Bolan's stock ace high in Jean-Paul's book.

The only tough spot, Bolan reflected, was choosing the moment when Raoul's attention was distracted so that he never got wise to the fact that the magazine Bolan slammed into the rifle wasn't the same one that the mobster himself had loaded.

The clip Bolan had shoved in—hidden until then in his pants pocket—carried only one live round and two blanks.

The live round shattered the glass roof of the assembly hall, all right. But it wasn't, as Bolan had said, to minimize the danger of deflection and make it easy for the next two: it was to tip off Telder that the operation was all systems go and alert his audience that something dramatic was on the way.

All the Interpol man had to do then, once he heard the distant reports of the second and third shot, was hurl himself backward against the wall behind the platform and press the gelatin ball concealed inside his jacket that so convincingly covered his chest with "blood."

The specially prepared ambulance would then rocket up to the school complex and whip the "body" away before professional medics could make it and blow the plan.

But apart from reinforcing his image as an ace contract artist, all this did was get Bolan off the hook for a while.

His score was zero so far on the seeds-of-discontent chart; he was not even sure what approach to take, what kind of discord to sow. And time was vitally short. Because of the attack on La Rocaille and the need for the expedition to Corsica, Antonin had agreed to wait a little longer for the final response, when the plan would be wrapped up for better or worse. But the Executioner had to start operating in a matter of days—perhaps even hours—if his own plan was to succeed.

What plan, Bolan thought wryly. It would be easier if he had one.

It was the day after Telder's "murder," and now Bolan sat above the sea in the Jaguar XJS he had been awarded as a bonus after that successful coup and pondered the problem. He was due to report at Jean-Paul's house, along with Smiler, Raoul, Bertrand, Delacroix and half a dozen other hoods in the early evening. Something had to be worked out—even if it was only in general terms—before then.

It was hot inside the low-slung car. The afternoon sunlight was glaring and fierce.

Mentally Bolan ran over the unrelated points he had filed away as potentially useful.

Jean-Paul was no birdbrain but he was an autocrat: he didn't go for anyone except himself making the decisions—and he could lose his cool if they did. The mobster from Marseilles was not one hundred percent certain that he could count on unstinting loyalty when the guy in question was the Corsican boss, Ancarani.

Ancarani himself, together with Lombardo, the capo who ran Toulon, and the Italian Scalese seemed slightly dubious of the KGB offer.

Smiler was an enemy, and would remain one, because Bolan had humbled him in front of his own men.

Raoul's sadism was likely to fog his judgment in a critical situation.

Coralie Sanguinetti blew hot and cold—but Bolan's gut reaction was that she would be on his side if she didn't regard him as a professional killer. And even believing that, she had thought enough of him to sense his mistrust of Antonin and fabricate an excuse to keep him out of the Russian's way.

Coralie was therefore likely to view any Russian participation—even indirectly—in her father's business with disfavor.

Could any of these disparate factors, proven and unproven, be threaded together strongly enough to fashion a cord? A cord that could be made into a noose?

Chain, Bolan thought, was a better image. A chain is really as strong as its weakest link, and there *were* weak links here.

The obvious one was the Ancarani-Scalese-Lombardo trio. Could their doubts be linked with Smiler's hostility and the temperamental idiosyncracies of Raoul and J-P himself in such a fashion that they threatened the balance of the coalition?

Bolan thought maybe they could.

But he would, after all, flip the problem back into the Pending tray until the meeting with the mobsters was through. Could be a more positive pointer would emerge there.

As for Coralie...well, she was the wild card!

Bolan fired up the Jaguar's V12, 225 horsepower engine. Backing the heavy speedster up onto the road, he lowered the visor against the setting sun and blasted off west, toward the city.

"This weekend," Jean-Paul said, "I don't have to tell you guys—it's the busiest of the whole year on the roads. Damn near the whole of France at the wheel: July vacationers going home; August families with kids on the way down here. Something like one hundred thousand automobiles on the move during these forty-eight hours!"

He paused and looked over his audience: Bolan and ten hardmen lounging in the white leather chairs that furnished the sun room overlooking the glittering sea those holidaymakers paid so much to be beside. Most of the mobsters wore puzzled expressions. "More than eighty percent of those folks," J-P explained, "will be using the north-south expressway. All of them will go through the pay station at Aix. Those driving down from Paris and Lyons will hand over six, seven bucks each. The ones heading home from Nice and Cannes will part with four or five at the tollbooths on the other side of town. Any of you smart enough to work out eighty thousand times five dollars?"

Delacroix, the giant who'd gotten burned during the Corsican raid, still wore bandages on his hands. Now the huge white paws rose and fell in a bewildered gesture. His simian brow furrowed in concentration. "Sure is a lotta bread," he agreed. "But I don't see what good that does us—I mean, with those armored trucks they have, the money is moved quicker'n fast. Ten minutes from the pay station an' it's in the vaults of the city bank."

"Not this weekend," J-P said. "The whole damn consignment, takings for both days, is going to Monte Carlo."

"Monte Carlo! But that's a hundred thirty miles!" one of the hoods exclaimed.

"That's right."

"Do you know this for sure?"

"Of course I know," snapped J-P. "Why do you think you're here? It's inside intel, from a contact in the bank."

"Okay, okay. But why...?"

"Something to do with a French government loan. The Monaco principality is supposed to be low on funds, so they want a big sum—in cash—to cover themselves in case the luck runs with the punters at the casino. I guess some smartass figured this was the quickest, easiest way to get it to them."

"And we're gonna hit the convoy transferring the loot?" Smiler asked.

"With more than one hundred miles of road to choose from? Damn right we are."

"Okay," the hood called Bertrand said. "But if we're about to shack up with the other mobs...if there's gonna be so much more bread flyin' around once the Comrades buy in...do we really need to take the risk? Or is this a joint operation?"

Jean-Paul shook his head. "No way. This is strictly a one-off. For us alone. As to why...well, it'll be a while before the arrangement with the Russians pays off. And in the meantime, we have a slight liquidity problem. It's only temporary but, among other things, that Corsican raid cost. In any case, it seemed too good a hit to miss, right? If any of you guys think it's a dumb idea..." He left the sentence unfinished.

Apparently nobody did. Bolan least of all because it had given him an idea of his own.

THE HEIST WAS WELL PLANNED and expertly carried out, Bolan had to admit. The site Jean-Paul had chosen was one of the tunnels that pierce the mountain mass above the ocean between Nice and the principality.

There were three advantages to the site. First, the expressway ran on the landward slopes of the mountain, and there were no towns or villages for several miles; second, the eastbound and westbound sections of the road were routed separately instead of sharing one wide tunnel; finally, the site chosen was only a couple of miles from the Monte Carlo turnoff, so the armed guards protecting the consignment would already be relaxing, figuring their trip was almost over.

Raoul, Bertrand, Smiler, Delacroix, Bolan and J-P himself were the inside men. Of the remaining six in the team, two were drivers and the other four had the task of removing the money.

Most of the money would be in bills equivalent to five and ten dollars, but there would be a sizeable amount in ten-franc coins, parceled in heavy sacks of one thousand. Smoothness and efficiency in the disposal of the loot was therefore going to be vital.

It was midafternoon when the armored truck with its four motorcycle outriders, two in front and two behind, approached the long upward grade that led to the tunnel. The cash would be in the casino strong room before the big-time roulette and baccarat players began to drift in at dusk.

It was a sultry day, the heat haze spreading inland from the sea and over the hills. Traffic was light. The tourists were either crowding the beaches or packing before they left their rented vacation villas and returned home. Most of the heavy commercial transport running between France and Italy had already passed.

But there was a forty-ton semi parked some way from the tunnel entrance on the emergency strip, with its hazard lights blinking. The driver was squatting by the front suspension, tightening something with a wrench. When the convoy was still several hundred yards away he climbed into his cab and the rig rumbled back onto the roadway and headed for the tunnel.

It was more than half a mile long. When the two leading bikers rode in out of the heat, the semi was still some way short of the exit. The armored truck and the other two cops followed. They were halfway through when it happened.

A sudden hiss of compressed air brakes...a squeal of rubber...and the front section of the huge truck skated across the roadway to graze the curved tunnel wall with a shriek of tortured steel. At the same time, the light, unloaded rear trailer jackknifed, swinging wide to hit the opposite wall and completely block the exit.

Double doors at the rear of the trailer had been flung open before the armored truck skidded to a halt and the two cops could draw their Brownings. From inside the trailer Jean-Paul and Delacroix fired heavy-caliber rubber bullets at the bikers, knocking them from their saddles. Simultaneously Bolan launched three gas grenades from an M-203 tube attached to an M-16 rifle—one between the fallen bikers, one beside the cab of the armored truck, the third toward the back of the vehicle, beneath the floor.

The fragile canisters were of a type unfamiliar to Bolan, but J-P had told him they should knock a man out for thirty minutes and leave no aftereffects.

They sure acted fast. Both cops were inert by the time Bolan and the two mafiosi, wearing gas masks and woolen balaclavas, thumped down the tailgate and raced toward the armored truck.

The gas, visible as faint wreaths of smoke in the yellow overhead lights illuminating the tunnel, coiled around the truck's cab. There was a driver and a guard armed with a Belgian FN machine pistol inside. But the windows were down because of the heat and both of them were out by the time the three hardmen sprinted up.

A third guard, similarly armed, would be in the back of the truck, with instructions not to come out under any circumstances, but to fire at once if anyone unauthorized tried to break in.

He wouldn't be coming out.

He wouldn't be firing when they broke in, either. There was a grill between the strong room and the cab, open too because of the heat, and a small ventilator revolving on the roof. Enough to allow in sufficient gas to render the guy unconscious.

There were ventilator fans also set in the tunnel roof, their five-foot blades designed to extract gasoline and diesel fumes. Buy they lay motionless now in the yellow light. The mobsters working outside had cut the current powering their motors and dismantled the blades minutes before the convoy was due.

Sensing trouble, the two cops riding shotgun had accelerated the moment they'd seen the semi blocking the exit. Passing the truck, they rode straight into the motionless gas cloud...and straight out of action, the BMW 650s toppling over and spinning to the tunnel walls as the cops slumped over their handlebars.

Bolan cut the fuel feed on all four roaring engines as J-P and the giant hauled the security men from the cab and searched them for keys.

A second semi was now broadsided across the roadway to block the tunnel's entrance. The driver, followed by Smiler and his two thugs, all of them wearing gas masks and balaclavas, ran to the stalled security vehicle. They were joined a moment later by the hood who had blocked the exit.

Everything now depended on timing. And it was here that Jean-Paul's organizational genius paid off. Instead of loading their haul into cars and attempting a getaway on one of the expressway lanes, instead of leaving the tunnel and making it across the countryside to another road, he had come up with a smarter idea.

The sabotaged fans in the roof, when they were working, pushed the extracted air up into shafts that penetrated the hillside and emerged into the open air 150 feet above the twin tunnels.

These shafts were thirty-six inches wide.

J-P stood now beneath one of them and blew three shrill blasts on a police whistle.

Seconds later a steel loader's hook on the end of a rope appeared at the shaft mouth in the tunnel roof. Rapidly it was lowered to the roadway. Working feverishly, Smiler and the other mobsters ransacked the armored truck, ranging boxes stuffed with bills and the heavy cylindrical coin sacks beneath the vent.

A second rope snaked down from the next shaft, fifty yards nearer the exit. Bolan, Raoul and Delacroix humped sacks and boxes over. Quickly now the hooks, loaded with three sacks at a time, rose upward and were swallowed in the darkness of the ventilator shafts, reappeared for another load, and then vanished again. On the hillside above two garage pickups equipped with powered hoists worked overtime.

It was a smart idea, all right. Bolan wondered with an inward grin just how much it had been influenced by his own ruse—as he had explained it to his boss—to get rid of the Husqvarna after the Telder "assassination."

Except for a few sacks of coins, the contents of the armored truck had been hoisted by the time the men in the tunnel heard the distant bray of police sirens. Bolan guessed that the guards, before the gas got to them, would have had time to send out an SOS.

"Okay, guys, that's it," Jean-Paul ordered at once. "We'll take the ropes ourselves now, two at a time."

While the first four men ran for the ropes, the others ranged the unconscious cops and guards alongside the plundered truck.

Jean-Paul had been insistent that on this deal there were to be no deaths. Mobsters and bribed police along the coast had reached an understanding. The mafiosi, handing out their hush money, could continue their protection rackets, the organization of cathouses and gambling joints, the distribution of drugs, the sacking of bank strong rooms—on condition.

There were to be no public shootouts; no hostage situations; no killings.

It would be exactly what the do-gooders wanted: The kind of thing that would bring the law down on the mafiosi at a critical time.

The shooting came later. And there were deaths, too.

Each of the two ropes came down twice; each time, four men were hoisted up the shafts to the surface. Bolan and J-P were on the final delivery—and already the horns of impatient drivers blocked outside the tunnel entrance were being drowned by the clamor of approaching sirens.

The air shafts emerged on a barren slope of sun drenched mountainside. The four mobsters manning the pickups had already begun stacking the haul around the hoists projecting over the open shafts. Now they maneuvered the vehicles back toward the dirt trail that had led them there. The path, made some years ago when the expressway was engineered, was too stony and overgrown for the cars that would carry away the hijackers and their spoils: these were parked on a loop of country road far below.

So were the attackers' vehicles—two jeeps and a 4x4 vehicle. But these were hidden behind a row of oaks, and the first the Marseilles gang knew of the assault was the burst of SMG fire that shattered the windshield of one of the pickups. Behind the crumbling glass the driver and Bertrand, who had climbed in beside him, were cut almost in two, leaving a pattern of blood and brains smeared over the back of the cab.

For a second the mobsters were stunned into immobility. Then the chatter of the gun was repeated from behind the pickup, followed at once by a volley of revolver shots.

Confusion.

Two more of the outside men were cut down, a third fell screaming with a slug through his kneecap, and the driver of the semi blocking the tunnel exit was hurled into the bushes by a heavy-caliber revolver bullet that slammed into his shoulder. Glass shattered and fell from the perforated cab of the second pickup.

"My God, it's a hijack!" Jean-Paul shouted. "Take cover and kill the bastards!" He flung himself behind a low shelf of rock, a Walther PPK in his right hand.

For the moment there was no target, visible or audible. The first volley seemed to have come from a group of boulders 150 yards uphill, on the far side of the trail, the second from below a limestone outcrop some way to the west. But so far no gunners had showed themselves.

Smiler, Delacroix and the others dived behind bushes, into a ditch beside the trail, among the rocks that littered the slope. Bolan was already prone beneath the first pickup, his Beretta in one hand, the M-16, its launcher discarded, by his side. He had been expecting the attack.

He was responsible for it.

The fact that the woolen helmets, covering the whole head except for the eyes, would make them unrecognizable had given him the idea.

All he had to do was arrange an anonymous tip off to Lombardo, the Toulon capo, that a bunch of free lance amateurs planned to ambush the armored convoy on Mafia territory.

And add the details of the getaway plan.

Fury at the interlopers' insolence—and greed at the thought of easy money—would surely provoke a hijack situation, Bolan figured.

So there would be an ambush. And whether or not Jean-Paul recognized the attackers while they were making their play, he would never believe that Lombardo had been ignorant of the original holdup teams' identity.

Open hostility, then, between these two leaders and their gangs.

As to who won the fight and made it with the loot...hell, it didn't really matter. Bitterness and suspicion would remain on both sides. With luck, some of the other teams, hearing of the screwup, would *take* sides and worsen the rift. It would do okay, Bolan thought, for a start....

He stared out from his hiding place. Jean-Paul's men were lightly armed. Because of his no-deaths ruling and the fact that they were using gas canisters, they had not expected any opposition; they hadn't expected any firefight at all.

The Marseilles mafioso's meager arsenal would not go far against a team armed with SMGs—Bolan figured them for Ingrams or Heckler & Kock MP-5s.

The element of surprise, too, had a demoralizing effect. Some of the guys from the tunnel hadn't even removed their gas masks when the first shots blasted off.

Jean-Paul himself was doing his damnedest. Three rounds cracked out from the Walther as a distant figure materialized between the boulders. There was a cry of pain. A stone rattled down the hillside toward the ambushed mobsters.

And then abruptly there was firing from all sides, a storm of lead hosing the pickups and the area around the ventilator shafts where the Marseilles soldiers were trapped.

The attackers were advancing now—silhouettes briefly seen as they leaped from bush to bush or wormed their way forward between the limestone outcrops.

Bolan snappped off a 3-round burst from the Beretta and saw a hoodlum fall. Slugs hailed against the steel sides of the pickup above the Executioner's head and stung rock splinters from the stony ground.

Smiler and Raoul blazed away from behind the other vehicle. Jean-Paul half rose and drilled a killer who tried to sprint down the trail. But the Marseilles chief was too slow ducking back behind his protecting shelf: a single shot from a rifle downhill dropped him. The Walther fell from nerveless fingers and skated into the center of the track.

But the marksman, making his hit, had himself been exposed. Bolan mowed him down with the M-16.

The big guy moved quickly then. On elbows and knees, the 93-R still in his right hand, he shuffled to the rock shelf were J-P had fallen.

The gang leader lay with outflung arms, the balaclava dark with blood. Bolan pulled off the woolen helmet. The white cap of hair was bloodied on one side. But Bolan soon discovered that the wound was not serious: The slug had merely creased the skull above the right ear, knocking the gang boss out cold.

"Is it bad?" the hoarse voice of Delacroix asked from the grasses on the far side of the trail.

"Uh-uh," Bolan replied. "He's out of the fight for now. But apart from a headache he'll be okay tomorrow and on his feet yelling blue murder the day after."

And not just because of the head wound, the Executioner thought. Then he glanced over the edge of the rock as he sensed movement. There were figures advancing again beyond the pickups. Sudden shapes, dark-clothed in the glaring light, flitting across the gaps between five-foot-high clumps of wild grass.

If they were moving, they couldn't fire accurately, Bolan reckoned. He made a quick dash back to the pickup, grabbed the M-16 and fired two bursts as the enemy came closer still and death hummed past on all sides.

He scored with both bursts. One of the ambushers fell, clawing at his shredded throat. Another gunman was carried backward by the impact of the high-velocity 5.56mm deathbringers that let the daylight into his rib cage.

The rate of firing increased once more. The air was shrill with ricochets.

Only five men remained now of the original Marseilles dozen: Smiler, Raoul, Delacroix, Bolan and the driver of the second semi.

"We're gonna have to pull out," Smiler growled from his foxhole nearby. "There must be ten of the bastards still on their feet."

Bolan said nothing. It was all the same to him. He'd play the cards the way they were dealt. The vital thing now was that the attackers should be recognized as Lombardo men. Maybe he should tempt one to come close enough...

He didn't have to.

Smiler was shouting orders. There was a flurry of activity, punctuated by bursts of rapid fire. The guy with the smashed kneecap was screaming again.

The remaining driver had gained the cab of the second pickup. Crouched below the dashboard, he had started the engine. Now, still huddled below the door line, he stomped the pedal and sent the pickup careering over the rough ground toward the trail.

Raoul and Smiler, unleashing all they had at the bushes concealing the attackers, leaped aboard on the near side and crammed into the cab. Delacroix, momentarily shielded by the bulk of the pickup, dragged the body of his unconscious leader from the ground, bundled him over the tailgate and then dived in after him as the vehicle gathered speed.

Bolan was left to race after the open truck, grab the side rails and vault over on his own. He had the impression that they would have left him behind if they could.

He lay panting beside the hoist, draped, like Delacroix and J-P, over the boxes and sacks that had already been loaded when the attackers opened fire. They were getting away with maybe one-third of the amount hauled up through the ventilator, leaving the bulk of the booty for Lombardo's thugs.

If they got away.

The pickup shuddered and screamed as lead thunked into the bodywork, caromed off the chassis and ribboned three of the tires.

The guy with the busted arm emerged from behind a boulder and lurched toward them, shouting something unintelligible over the crackle of fire. Bolan and Delacroix slammed in fresh clips and tried to cover him, but the wounded hood never had a chance. He fell on his knees in the dust, choking out his lifeblood as the words ended in a bubbling scream, riddled by slugs from half a dozen guns.

The driver was sitting upright now, wrestling with the wheel, struggling to keep the pickup—limping and screeching on three steel rims—running straight along the track.

"What about Louis?" the driver asked as they slalomed toward the rock where the soldier with the shattered knee was lying.

"Fuck him," Smiler grated. "Get us the hell outta here."

It was ten boneshaking yards later that the nickel dropped. Passing the slope of rock where Bolan had downed a man, Raoul glanced below the gory trail to where the dead hood's face stared sightlessly up from the grasses. "Jeez!" he gasped. "That's...it can't be, but—hell, that's *Lombardo* there!"

"No way," Smiler snapped. "How could it be?"

"It is. I swear it. But what the *hell*...?"

Perhaps fortunately it was Smiler himself who witnessed the clincher. The driver swung wide to skate past the body of the man Jean-Paul had dropped in the middle of the trail. And now it was Smiler's turn to stare.

"Sonovabitch," he breathed again, "you're goddamn right: that's Michel Calvet, one of Lombardo's soldiers!" He shook his head and then muttered between clenched teeth: "The double crossing bastards!"

On the whole, Bolan thought as they clattered away and then down toward the parked automobiles and safety, not a bad afternoon's work....

14

In his office high above the lake in Geneva, Colonel Mathieu Telder took three pieces of paper from a brown manila envelope and spread them on his desk between the two telephones.

The papers were news clippings. He read them slowly, a slight smile on his lips.

The first was the longest. It had been clipped from the main news page of *Nice-Matin* and gave details of the daring tunnel raid and subsequent shootout on the hillside west of La Turbie.

Telder put the cutting aside and picked up the second. It was much shorter. Taken from an inside page of that day's *France-Soir*, the two-inch news item recounted a bombing incident that wrecked a bar frequented by criminals in the dock quarter of Toulon the previous night. The attack, Telder read, was thought to be a "reprisal" for the hijack that followed the daring $500,000 "tunnel holdup" with the loss of ten lives. The story stated that three men had been killed and a fourth was missing after the explosion, which was thought to have been caused by a suitcase bomb left under a table in the bar.

The dead were all associates of the late Pasquale Lombardo.

Telder glanced only briefly at the third clipping. He was already familiar with the contents: he had himself supplied the background information for the story. It reported that police frogmen dragging a flooded chalk pit outside Marseilles had recovered the body of Maître Gaspard Delpêche, a well-known defense attorney who had been missing for some days. The lawyer had been shot once in the nape of the neck.

Readers were reminded that a second prominent citizen of the city, the columnist Georges Dassin, was also missing and must be presumed dead; that the body of the popular television personality, Michel Lasalle, had been found floating in the ocean; and that a high official of Interpol, a guest of the city government, had only a few days before been cold-bloodedly gunned down at a public meeting.

A spokesman for the police described the recent increase in violent crime in the area as "intolerable and wholly unacceptable."

Telder grinned. He hoped the subjects of the story appreciated its irony in the safety of their reluctant hideouts.

Bolan was doing all right, anyway. The forces of law and order along the coast would have at least to make a pretense of acting...and that would add to the instability of the Mafia situation whether or not they actually got around to busting anyone.

The Interpol chief nodded in satisfaction now as he thought of the Executioner. The American warrior was risking everything—his life—to thwart the planned coalition between the KGB and the Mafia in Europe. So far the soldier's strategy—whatever it was—seemed to be working fine, and Telder had a feeling that before the Executioner was finished, the Red menace would cover the land. The threat would not be from the Russians, however. Instead it would be spilled Mafia blood.

15

Bolan swung the Jaguar off the highway and parked it discreetly in a multistory parking lot on the outskirts of Civitaveccia, forty miles west and north of Rome. He took a cab to the town center and walked to the docks.

It was a blisteringly hot day and the tourists on the waterfront were dressed in the minimum, but Bolan wore a spotless white coverall that sheathed him from wrist to ankle. Stitched to the breast pocket was a yellow shield bearing a rampant horse in red, with the word Ferrari above it. To complete a picture immediately identifiable by any Italian, he had allowed a day-old haze of stubble to blue his jaw.

A freighter from Marseilles had docked early in the morning, and its cargo was being unloaded. Among the merchandise was an automobile. It belonged to Baron Etang de Brialy, the Parisian underworld boss, who was to take delivery of it in Rome the following day and then drive south to Reggio de Calabria on the Strait of Messina.

From here, along with the other Mafia chiefs, he was to be ferried in a private yacht, not to Sicily but to the island of Stromboli, where Sanguinetti owned another property.

After the intensive newspaper, radio and television coverage of the past few days' excesses, all hell had broken loose along the Riviera coast, and Jean-Paul had figured it would be tempting fate to reorganize a gathering of so many high powered Mafia men in one place until the heat was off.

Italy and Sicily were out of the question since Tommaso Buscetta, late in 1984, had broken the Law of Silence and blown half the Mafia operations there and in the United States so wide open that all the law had to do was step in and snap on the handcuffs.

An island in the middle of the ocean, with no roads, no police and no regular transport service to the mainland seemed an ideal place to thrash out the final terms of the amalgamation with Colonel Antonin.

Bolan, Smiler, Raoul and Delacroix, together with a score of side men owing allegiance to other bosses, were to make their own way to Reggio di Calabria.

Right now, Bolan was ahead of schedule. He had gained twelve hours by driving through the night instead of stopping off to eat and sleep at a motel. During those twelve hours he intended to "borrow" Etang de Brialy's car, use it on a private operation, and then continue on south in his own Jaguar.

The car was a 400 hp, twin-turbo Ferrari GTO, a sleek road racer whose center-mounted 3.8 liter V8 engine could power the car from 0 to 60mph in 4.8 seconds.

The 190 mph roadster was painted lemon yellow with a broad black stripe running from the nose, over the squat roof to the stubby tail. With Paris license plates, it was not the kind of vehicle to escape attention, even in race-mad Italy, the home of supercars. That suited the Executioner just fine.

There were gasps of admiration from dockers and tourists alike as the Ferrari was swung from the freighter's hold and lowered gently to the wharf. Nobody thought for a moment to dispute Bolan as an official driver from the Ferrari factory at Maranello when he strode forward, unsmiling, and waited for the longshoremen to free the five-spoke alloy wheels from their chains.

Owner's instructions were to park the car in a dockside lot and leave the keys with the harbormaster, from whom Etang de Brialy's driver would collect them the following morning. But nobody questioned Bolan's authority when he said that plans had been changed: he was to deliver the car to the Baron in Rome immediately. A fistful of 10,000-lire bills distributed left and right served to validate his authenticity further still.

Bolan sank into the perforated black leather driving seat and twisted the key. There was a momentary hum from the roadster's Weber-Marelli injection system, and then the engine crackled to life. Bolan raised a languid hand in farewell and allowed the Ferrari to rumble slowly toward the dock gates.

He drove south until he hit the outskirts of Rome, by-passing the city on the parkway that circled the center. On the famous southern expressway beyond, he floored the pedal and howled up through the gears until the tachometer's red needle was nudging the 7,500 rpm danger line. Then, easing the stick into fifth, he settled down the low, wide sportster at just over 150 mph and prepared to enjoy ride.

It was an exhilarating experience. Bolan was a skillful driver and his big hands, tweaking the three-branched wheel only fractionally as the Ferrari streaked past the lunchtime traffic, held the car steady as an arrow in flight.

Behind his head the throaty aspirations of the inter-cooled IHI turbochargers, the whine and chatter of thirty-two valves and twin overhead camshafts mingled with the bellow of exhaust from the big-bore tailpipes to exult in the achievement of man the engineer.

Bolan wished he could leave it at that. But it was man the animal that his business was with. The Camorra, he had read, was believed to be behind a nationwide child prostitution racket in Italy, a scandal that involved boys as well as girls. It was a subject on which he found it hard to keep his cool.

His own crusade against the Mafia had started after a compassionate repatriation from Nam had brought him face-to-face with murder and suicide in his own family. And that had been the direct consequence of his kid sister's turning whore in a desperate attempt to find enough cash to pay off Mafia loan sharks.

Bolan shook his head sadly. Sure, the battleground changed, but the story remained the same. And it would, he knew, always *be* the same. But while he was alive, he'd do his best to change the plot. And with any luck he could at the same time toss another wrench into the proposed alliance of the KGB and European Mafia.

Valmontone, Montecassino and Caserta dropped behind the roaring Ferrari. Soon the *autostrada* looped down toward Naples and the impossibly blue bay beyond. The Ferrari GTO had made the 129 miles from Rome in exactly one hour.

Bolan drove south of the sinister cone of Vesuvius, left the expressway at Castellammare, and piloted the car around the mountainous hairpins of the Sorrento peninsula.

Girolamo Scalese, the Camorra boss, lived in a huge white villa high above the ocean between Positano and Amalfi. Bolan approached it from behind, crossing the ridge on Route 366, and parking the Ferrari some way from the gates. He wanted the car to be seen and recognized but he did not wish it to be damaged.

The villa, built around a central patio big enough to accommodate a jumbo-size pool, was shaded by palms. It was surrounded by stone terraces brilliant with geraniums and purple bougainvillea. An arch in the twelve-foot stone wall enclosing the property was filled by electrically operated wooden gates with a small window.

Vines clung to the hillside east of the house, and beyond these there was a view of Amalfi, the pastel-colored buildings set into the cliff like bright books on shelves.

Bolan stared down at the glitter of expensive cars along the coast road, the sprinkle of beach umbrellas on the volcanic ash shore, the white patterns etched by pleasure boats into the distant azure heave of the ocean. He shook his head.

Too bad that the slime-bucket scum who could afford to live in a place like this had acquired it through exploitation, intimidation and corruption.

If he played it right, perhaps they would be sorry they did live here.

Wearing his blacksuit now, he eased himself out of the Ferrari's cockpit and walked to the gates of Scalese's property.

The sun beat fiercely on his face, half blinding him where it glared off the sea. In the center of the roadway the macadam, softening in the heat, sucked at the soles of his shoes.

He had decided on the frontal approach. The wall was topped with broken glass and there would certainly be sensors, electrified alarm wires and probably killer dogs on the far side. A wrought-iron bellpull hung from a bracket beside the gates. He jerked it and heard a jangle someplace inside.

The window snapped back and a brutish, heavy-jawed face stared out. "Whatta we got here?" the gateman exclaimed, seeing Bolan's black-clad figure. "Batman?"

"Superman," Bolan said evenly. "I want to see Scalese."

"On your way, smartass. Nobody gets to see the boss."

"I have a message for him from Renato Ancarani. Personal," Bolan said.

"Phone it in. You ought to know that nobody—"

"Your phone's tapped by the *carabinieri*."

"Bullshit. The boss pays good money he should keep his line free of snoopers."

"He didn't pay enough. This is important."

"So is privacy." The gorilla was scowling. "Now beat it." The window slammed shut.

Bolan walked to the Ferrari. Sixty seconds later he was back. He rang the bell again.

The window opened. The gateman's face was red with anger. Before he could speak, Bolan said swiftly, "I got credentials." He held up an envelope in his left hand.

Still scowling, the hood leaned his face near the opening, squinting at the envelope. "What credentials?"

"These," Bolan said. With fingers splayed, his right hand shot forward with lightning speed, temporarily blinding the man, the impact of the blow also stunning him.

There was a high-pitched whinnying noise and the face vanished. Bolan reached for the grappling hook and the coil of rope he had brought from the car. He swung the hook over the gates. Seconds later he dropped lightly down from the arch inside the entrance.

The gatekeeper was writhing on the ground, clutching his face and whimpering like a baby.

Bolan unleathered Sondermann's Beretta, silenced now, from its shoulder rig and sent it crashing along the side of the man's head. He stopped moaning and Bolan dragged the body out of sight behind a clump of palmettoes.

He had reasoned that the gateway, being guarded all the time, would be free of sensor beams. Evidently he had been right, for no other hardmen appeared. He glanced swiftly around.

Between walled terraces covered in exotic shrubs a flagged driveway curled away and then dived beneath the house to an open four-car garage containing a Silver Shadow Rolls-Royce, an Alfa Romeo sportster and a large station wagon. With his back to the entrance a heavyset man wearing nothing but jeans was polishing the Rolls.

Bolan holstered the Beretta. Keeping to the inside of the curve, he sidled as near as he could before making his move. He was eight feet from the open doors when the guy looked up.

"What the hell...?"

Bolan rocketed forward and launched a flying jump kick at the chauffeur's jaw. The man backed off but not quickly enough: half the force of the Executioner's blow was expended by the time it homed in, lower down, on the guy's chest, but it was enough to knock him back against the big limo's hood. For an instant he sprawled and then, as Bolan landed on the balls of his feet, he squared off and adopted a karate position, one arm held out, the other close in to the body.

Okay, Bolan thought. We play it your way. He could have finished it with the silenced gun but the cold fury that had fueled his actions ever since he read of the Camorra child racket still seethed within him: his gut reaction was to kill with his bare hands.

The mafioso attacked first. A feint to one side, and then a double heel-of-the-hand assault aimed at the temples. Bolan parried it with upthrust forearms, jumped back and thudded in a crossbody *shuto* stroke as the man lurched forward.

The chauffeur gasped, reeling against the Alfa. But he pushed himself away before Bolan could spring and launched a deadly *seiken* punch, a ram's head blow with all his weight behind it, that caught the Executioner over the heart and sent him down.

Bolan rolled as a heavy kick caught him in the ribs. He was halfway to his feet when his adversary ran in with a tae kwon do kick to the head. Bolan dropped back, seizing the out-thrust foot as it streaked toward him. He twisted it and sent the guy hurtling on, propelled by his own impetus, to crash against the wall and slide to the floor.

Shaking his head groggily, he pushed himself upright and advanced menacingly, one fist held cocked for a murderous roundhouse punch that was designed to kayo Bolan for good.

Bolan rode it, dropped a high side kick to the sphenoid and then, as the hood staggered, finished it with another slashing *shuto* stroke to the throat. The plank-hard edge of his hand smashed his opponent's windpipe. The chauffeur fell, gargling his own blood.

Bolan ran for the stairway leading to the villa from the back of the garage.

The fight hadn't been too noisy, but the dying chauffeur had twice been thrown against an automobile and that must have been enough to alert the two gorillas catfooting down toward him.

One carried a leather-covered blackjack; the other was hefting a Beretta like Bolan's. He looked as if he knew how to use it, but the Executioner's gun spoke before the guy could press the trigger—a 3-round burst more discreet than the popping of champagne corks. More lethal, too.

He wristed the auto-loader from right to left, as he triggered the trio of skullbusters. One shot was wasted: the slug gouged a chip from the concrete stair between the two men. The other two scored five on five, tumbling the two hardmen and engraving a crimson abstract on the white wall as they fell.

Bolan spread his arms, catching the two bodies before he lowered them silently to the floor. He made the top of the stairs and found himself in a short passage leading through to the patio. Passing an empty kitchen gleaming with copper and stainless steel, he paused at the patio doorway and looked across the pool at a girl stretched out sunbathing on a striped mattress.

He tiptoed back to the kitchen. A vacuum cleaner was parked just inside. He unscrewed the hose with its chromed metal tip and carried it back to the open doorway.

The doorway was in deep shadow, the patio outside vibrating in the hot glare of the sun. Bolan balanced the hose on a bookshelf just inside the doorway, arranging it so that the metal tip projected a couple of inches out from the shadow.

He approached the girl from behind. She was lying on her back with her eyes closed, a tall empty glass nearby. She sat up with a gasp when his shadow fell across her face—a platinum blonde with long tapering legs and a bronzed body the color of polished olive wood. She was wearing the briefest of bikinis in silver satin.

Bolan gestured with the gun. "Don't make a sound," he warned. "Walk over there and get into the pool."

Her eyes were wide with terror. "I...I can't swim."

"You don't have to. Stay at the shallow end."

"No, but...my swimsuit will get wet. It will be ruined."

She flicked an apprehensive glance over her right shoulder.

Bolan followed her movement and saw a blue canvas awning under which double glass doors led to another part of the villa. That must be where the big shot was holed up, Bolan guessed.

"Look," he murmured, "I'm in a hurry. All you have to do is get in the pool and sit in the shallow end with just your head showing." He looked across the pool.

"But if you step out of line my partner over there will see you." He pointed to the tip of the vacuum hose where it gleamed out of the shadow. "That's a cannon he has there. One squawk out of you, and he'll blow your pretty head away. Okay?"

Wordlessly, trembling, she went to the ladder and lowered herself into the tepid water.

Bolan found Scalese in a bright, airy room with picture windows overlooking the sea. He was wearing a flowered Hawaiian shirt and white shorts above thin tanned legs. His silver hair was crimped close to his skull and his face was as lined as a yellowed sheet of music.

The Executioner took in the inlaid Renaissance cabinets, nineteenth century oil paintings, a tiger-skin rug, before the gang boss spoke.

"What's happen? Who are you? How the hell you get inna here?" He was holding an unlit cigar. He didn't seem angry, only faintly surprised.

"The racket," Bolan said grimly. "The kid prostitute racket. You're the brains behind it, the guy places the orders, right?"

Scalese picked a gold cigar cutter from a desk and guillotined his Corona. "So what of it?" he said, shrugging.

"In Paris," Bolan said carefully, "we don't go for that. The baron does not approve."

"Whatsa matter wit' you? You crazy or something?" The sallow forehead corrugated even more as Scalese's eyebrows rose. "It's no business of his. Or yours. What do I care for Paris? I run my family the way I want."

"If we're going into business together, *we* wouldn't want to be associated with the kind of scum who seeks out deprived kids, tempts them with offers of money, exploits them—" the words trembled in Bolan's mouth "—and then ruins them for life."

"You tell your baron he go fuck himself. So what if a few punk kids get laid a coupla years early? They'll be on their backs soon enough, anyway, and this way they getta some money, too. What so corrupt in that, tell me?"

Bolan had seen the surreptitious jab at the desk button when Scalese picked up his cigar cutter, was aware of the turning spools of the tape deck beneath the windows: if they were being recorded he wanted the connection between the baron, the yellow Ferrari and what was going to happen to Scalese to be clear. "The Baron won't stand for that kind of filth."

"Say, how did you get in here, anyway?" Scalese asked.

"You need better security," Bolan said.

The Camorra boss turned back to the desk and picked up a small bronze conversation piece, a shepherd leaning over a tree stump. The shepherd's head had been cut and hinged to accommodate a cigarette lighter. "I hope you don' hurt none of my boys getting through." He swung around to face Bolan, raised the statuette level with his chest and flicked the lighter. He held the flame to his cigar.

Bolan was alert for any sudden moves. He was off the mark and diving the instant the hidden shutter opened in the base of the bronze piece.

The deadly steel dart ripped the lobe of his ear as it hurtled past him. Bolan rammed Scalese's chest with his shoulder and carried the two of them back over the polished top of the desk. A black letter case, an inkwell, a jeweled paper knife and a Venetian ashtray crashed to the floor. The two men landed in a heap beneath the windows.

Scalese was quick for his age. A stiletto was already in his hand as he twisted out from under the Executioner. But anger had fueled Bolan's strength and determination. Ignoring the menace of that flickering point, he went straight for the man's arm.

The blade slashed the strap of his shoulder rig, pricked blood through the sleeve of his blacksuit and scratched his hand before his fingers closed in on the bony wrist.

Violently, he jerked the arm down against an upthrust knee. The weapon clattered away; the bone snapped dryly as a dead branch in winter.

Scalese screamed.

Bolan picked him up by his ankles and swung him. He whirled the mafioso around like an Olympic athlete winding up a hammer throw, then crashed the old man's head against one of the picture windows.

Scalese's skull shattered the glass. The pane exploded with a jangling concussion.

Once more Bolan swiveled. At the completion of the turn, he hurled the Camorra chief savagely out through the broken window.

Blood laced the air as Scalese's ribboned body dropped fifteen feet in a cascade of razor-sharp fragments to a terrace planted with olives and fruit trees.

He lay groaning feebly, with streams of scarlet fanning out from his broken body to sink into the sunbaked earth. Even if he lived, Girolamo Scalese wasn't going to be propositioning underage kids for quite some time.

Bolan turned back into the room. A swarthy gorilla in a cream-colored suit was standing in the doorway, his right hand diving between his lapels.

In one fluid movement Bolan scooped up the fallen paper knife by the point and thrust it with murderous aim at the hood. The sharp blade sank into the guy's throat and he subsided to the floor with a bubbling moan.

Bolan jumped over the body and raced for the patio. Another mobster, attracted by the noise of smashing glass, was running along the passage toward Bolan. The big guy wasted him as he ran, a single shot from the Beretta impacting below his breastbone, pulverizing liver and spleen.

On the far side of the patio, between Scalese's quarters and the kitchen wing, three more hoods were approaching the Executioner. The girl was still in the pool, her blond hair and frightened face incongruous above the surface of the blue water.

"Keep your head down!" Bolan yelled.

He unhitched a small plastic grenade from the blacksuit harness, pulled the pin and threw it across the pool.

A momentary flash dimmed the blaze of the sun. A cracking thunderclap of an explosion. More glass shattered and fell. Masonry dropped and broken tiles slid into the patio from the roof.

A shower of blood stained the walls.

Bolan reholstered the Beretta. "You can come out now," he told the blonde. "Don't look behind you…and get the hell out of here."

He walked around to the kitchen passage and descended the stairs to the garage.

At the end of the driveway he pressed the button to open the electrically operated gates and regained the Ferrari.

Turning the roadster so that he could go back the way he had come, he backed up into the villa entrance. The hood with the paper knife in his throat could still be alive; there might be other guys on Scalese's payroll in other rooms; the girl might be watching. Whatever, he wanted to be quite sure somebody saw him leaving in that yellow-and-black car.

With their reports, and the evidence on the tape, whether Scalese himself lived or died, Baron Etang de Brialy was going to have a lot of explaining to do when the story broke on his arrival on Stromboli.

And nobody was going to believe some fool story about his Ferrari having been stolen. Not when it would be found tomorrow right where it should be, in the dockside parking lot, with the keys in the harbormaster's office!

Bolan wore a satisfied smile as he floored the pedal, heading for Naples and Rome.

16

Sanguinetti's yacht was in the Onassis class. Below the streamlined stack that funneled the vapors from its twin 1200 hp diesels into the sky, three promenade decks accommodated a dining room, a lounge, a bar and sleeping quarters for thirty-two people. Two of the latest powered self-righting lifeboats were stowed aft of the wheelhouse and bridge, and there was a small helipad with a Dassault chopper above the crew's mess hall.

Perhaps in ironic allusion to his own name—or even to the activities of his friends—Sanguinetti had christened his sixty-million-dollar status symbol *Bloody Mary*.

Neither the richness of the appointments nor the elegance of *Bloody Mary*'s thoroughbred line drew Mack Bolan's attention after he had left the Jaguar in Reggio and come aboard on the afternoon of the day following his visit to Scalese. It was something much more mundane that attracted him to the luxuriously equipped bar on the upper promenade deck.

A giant-screen television set sat above the rows of bottles and glasses.

He had heard the initial news flash on the car radio, but he was anxious for the fuller version that TV would provide. And there it was! Seven people were dead and a dozen injured after a street battle in downtown San Francisco.

Gunmen from the East Coast had invaded the city's dock area in a fleet of cars and shot up local racketeers in a running battle that had lasted more than an hour. Among the dead was an underworld boss named Luigi Abba.

A handful of mobsters sprawling in the soft seats around the bar stopped drinking long enough to comment jeeringly on the bulletin. "Just like old times," one of them guffawed. "Hey, Sondermann, is that the way they run things where you come from, too?"

"At least we try to keep our private quarrels off the TV screen," Bolan said.

A dispute over Mafia "territory" was thought to be at the root of the dispute, the newscaster said. Vincente Borrone, one of the leading New York mafiosi, was being held as a material witness although he denied any knowledge of the affair.

Bolan took in the pictures of bullet-riddled sedans and the chalked sidewalk outlines of corpses and nodded with satisfaction.

He looked out beyond the forested masts and rigging of the harbor, to the open sea that lay on the far side of the narrow passage separating Reggio de Calabria from Sicily.

Stromboli and the seven other islets comprising the Lipari group were forty nautical miles away. With the power churned out by *Bloody Mary*'s twin screws, they should be there in less than two hours.

There would be absences, though. Apart from Borrone and Abba. Bolan figured from his knowledge of the mob scene Stateside that the bosses from Chicago, Detroit—and maybe New Orleans and Florida, as well—would be too anxious to put their weight behind the remnants of Abba's gang, too busy trying to chisel themselves a piece of the action, to make the trip. Barrone's nationwide stranglehold on the organization was not popular.

Still, it was kind of ironic—the Executioner permitted himself a grim smile—the role he himself was playing.

Instead of his usual hellfire attacks, his anti-Mafia tactics here were based on thinking that paralleled the worldwide strategy favored by the KGB: precisely in the style of that evil organization, having laid his plans, he was standing aside and allowing his adversaries to destroy themselves from the inside!

Bolan didn't know it, but he wasn't going to be allowed to remain on the sidelines much longer.

MARCEL SANGUINETTI'S PROPERTY on Stromboli satisfied the same desire for privacy that was apparent at La Rocaille. It was separated from the houses of the island's one poor fishing village by a low headland of black volcanic basalt that ran out under the sea.

The villa was in the style peculiar to the islands: square, flat roofed, spread over many terraces and approached beneath an arbor of grapevines supported on lime washed masonry pillars. A rough track led there from the village: the arbor was directed toward an expensive landing stage.

The volcano on the island, no more than three thousand feet high, is active, liable to erupt at any time.

As they neared the island, the boatload of mafiosi saw with some trepidation that a wisp of dark smoke curled upward from the crater.

"Hell," a minor mobster from Marseilles exclaimed. "The bastard's gonna puke hot rocks and bury us all!"

"Nah!" commented one of the bodyguards accompanying Zefarelli, the Sicilian chief. "She's always blowin' a little steam—nothing to worry about."

Some of the hoods laughed. One or two looked as dubious as the guy from Marseilles. Otto Schuyler, a hood from Amsterdam who had not been at the original meeting in Marseilles, scowled and spat on the floor. "Hell, I thought this was supposed to be a goddamned get-together of guys with guts," he sneered.

Bolan listened to the interplay and wondered what was the best way to capitalize on such paranoia that it would complete the disintegration he himself had started.

Right now, he had to let the subject drop. There was a long rattling rumble as *Bloody Mary* dropped anchor.

Jean-Paul walked into the bar with Sanguinetti and the Sicilian boss. "Okay, you guys," he called, "break it up. We're going ashore."

ANTONIN'S CHOPPER WAS DUE before dusk. Before that, Coralie Sanguinetti, who had arrived on the island the previous day, organized an open air meal prepared and served by locals, on a huge patio.

It was suffocatingly hot on that windless afternoon. The sun glared from a sky the color of hammered pewter, the sea scarcely stirred and the wisp of smoke veiling Stromboli's crater remained motionless.

Jean-Paul had decided to deliver a last-minute pep talk on the necessity for a united front. He strode up and down among the senior mafiosi—Bolan, along with strongarm men, was being fed in an adjoining courtyard—brandishing a leg of cold chicken as he urged the vital importance of total agreement.

He was emphasizing how essential it was for Antonin to be convinced that there was not the slightest hint of discord, when the clatter of an approaching helicopter floated over the murmur of voices around the patio.

Almost at once the rotor whine was itself drowned out
by the rasp of a powerboat surging in toward Sanguinetti's private landing.

For an instant Jean-Paul paused, and then he resumed
his harangue. He had hardly spoken when hurrying footsteps echoed along the stone walk beneath the arbor that
led from the harbour.

Two thickset men burst onto the patio, each carrying a
Walther PPK automatic. One of them wore a white hos-
pital bandage around his neck.

Through the archway separating the two courtyards,
Bolan recognized the hood whose throat he had pierced
with the paper knife. The other guy looked as though he
could be Scalese's son. Surreptitiously Bolan checked that
the Beretta slid easily in its leather.

Jean-Paul stopped in midspeech. "What the *hell*...?"

"What kind of shit are you bastards trying to pull?" the
guy who looked like Scalese's son shouted. "Where the
hell does this mother get off—" the two men surged toward Jean-Paul, furious and menacing "—sending in his
goddamn gorilla to break up my old man's place, trying to
crease the old guy?"

"All right. Cool it, damn you." Two angry spots of
color burned on J-P's cheeks. "What do you mean by
busting in here like this! Who the hell are you talking
about?"

"De Brialy, that's who," Scalese Jr. yelled. "Where is
the creep? I'll tear him to pieces!"

Pandemonium all around the patio. Some of the hoods
were protesting, some laughed, some stood up to see better. There was a sudden increase of noise as the helicopter
passed low over the villa and hovered above the landing
stage.

De Brialy rose slowly to his feet, small, prim, gray. "Just what exactly am I supposed—" he began.

"My old man may not live: his skull is cracked, his bones are broken, he's all busted up inside," Scalese raved. "Seven of his housemen are wasted. And all because of some crap relating to cathouse kids. Don't deny it, you frog bastard: it's all on the tape."

The guy with the bandaged throat obviously found it too painful to speak, but he nodded violently, gesturing with his gun at Etang de Brialy. One or two of the mafiosi had unobtrusively circled behind the two intruders and now they were covered on all sides.

Jean-Paul sighed. "Maybe it would be better if we continued this indoors," he said.

Together with the two enraged Italians, Etang de Brialy and a handful of the other capos, he hurried toward a colonnade running outside Sanguinetti's quarters along one side of the patio.

Passing the arch that led to the second courtyard, Scalese's companion looked up and saw Bolan sitting among the gorillas. He froze, tugging at Scalese's sleeve as he croaked something unintelligible in a raucous ghost of a voice. Scalese whirled. "That dude? He's the bastard did the job?"

Bandaged-throat nodded, his own eyes murderous.

The barrel of the PPK swung up.

"Cut that out!" Hard as a plank, J-P's hand chopped down on Scalese's wrist, knocking the gun to the ground. At the same time Etang de Brialy twisted the other Walther away from the bandaged hood.

"This is a time for talking, not shooting," the Marseillais rapped sharply. He glanced up as a shadow swept across the patio. Swooping low above the building, Antonin's chopper was about to set down. "And a damned awkward time it is," Jean-Paul muttered.

He looked across at the inner courtyard. "Sondermann, you'd better come along, too, until we get this whole mess sorted out."

Bolan was already on his feet. Time for the showdown, yeah, just as he had expected. He flipped open the single button of his jacket for easier access to the shoulder rig, but from behind two hands closed in on his biceps and Smiler's voice drawled: "Not so fast, Fritz. I always did think there was something creepy about you. Now I smell a rat—a rat with a not-quite-strong-enough German accent."

Chuckling to himself, Raoul snared the Beretta from its armpit rig and the two of them marched Bolan indoors after the others. "Better for the boss he should be in no danger when he gets wise," Smiler rasped.

Inside the villa they crowded into a wide, low-ceilinged room with huge windows looking out onto a terrace of black volcanic ash planted with orange and lemon trees. The branches of the trees thrashed as the helicopter settled down between the terrace and the landing stage.

Jean-Paul stood with his back to a vast marble chimneypiece. The remainder of the mafiosi stood awkwardly among the cane tables and chaise longues furnishing the room.

"Okay," Jean-Paul said tightly. "Now let's have it. One guy at a time. One idea at a time. And it better be good." He turned to the Camorra boss's son. "Scalese?"

Before the young man could reply, Otto Schuyler, the Dutchman, erupted into the room. "Just a minute!" he shouted. "Did I hear you call this guy Sondermann? Kurt Sondermann, from Hamburg?" He strode up to Bolan and stared into his face. "Well, you're being taken for a ride. This ain't Sondermann. I know the dude: I worked with him. There's a resemblance, sure, but this ain't him!''

There was a sudden silence in the room. Bolan tensed.

The grip on his biceps tightened. "Here's where you get yours, asshole," Smiler's voice snarled gleefully in his ear.

Jean-Paul stepped forward. His eyes had a puzzled look. Obviously he was recalling Bolan's help during the tunnel raid, his support in the fight with Lombardo that followed, the four hits he had carried out. He seized the lapels of the Executioner's jacket.

"If you're not Sondermann, who the hell are you? And you have one chance to come across with the truth...."

Jean-Paul paused, looking over his shoulder.

Footsteps clacked along the stone corridor leading from the room to the villa gardens. Dimitri Alexsandrevitch Antonin stood in the doorway, resplendent in the dress uniform of a colonel in the KGB, his shaven head gleaming in the dim light.

He took in the scene at a glance, frowned and then centered his gaze on the group before the chimneypiece and in particular on the tall, muscled guy held by Jean-Paul and his two henchmen.

This time his eyes widened in recognition.

"What the devil are you doing with that man here?" he shouted. "How did he get in? Don't you have any sense at all, any of you? That's the capitalist mercenary, Mack Bolan."

17

"Bolan!" It was clear from Jean-Paul's stupefied voice that the name meant plenty to him. He fell back a pace, half releasing his grip. As he opened his mouth to speak again, a long, shivering tinkle agitated all the china on the chimneypiece behind him.

The air in the room trembled. The ground shook.

There was a continuous, low rumbling roar that crescendoed in a distant explosion. It was followed by another.

The volcano on Stromboli was flexing its muscles.

For a moment there was silence in the big crowded room. Then everyone began to speak, some denouncing Bolan, others concerning Antonin, most of them scared by the eruption.

Coralie Sanguinetti ran in from the servant's wing. "Papa," she said breathlessly, "it's spitting fire up there. There's a huge cloud of black smoke, with sparks and flames underneath. Maria and Giancarlo and the others are frightened; they want to go back to the village."

"Let them go—" Bolan had not noticed the industrialist before: he was sitting in a cane chair by the windows "—they should be familiar enough with Stromboli by now: no harm will come to them."

The brunette stared at him for a moment, glanced briefly at the tableau that had Mack Bolan as its centerpiece and then left the room.

"Well, Bolan? If that is who you are?" Jean-Paul resumed as though there had been no interruption. "Like I said: I want an explanation."

He stepped forward and struck the Executioner viciously across the face, backhand and forehand, with the full sweep of his arm. The blows were strong enough to rock the big guy's head on his shoulders and leave livid welts marking his cheeks. But he remained rigid in the grip of J-P's two goons, staring unflinchingly and expressionlessly at the gang boss.

"I don't like people who try to make a fool out of me," Jean-Paul growled. "That's something you're gonna regret for sure. But before you suffer, believe me, you're gonna sing."

At Bolan's ear there was a shrill, infantile giggle. "He's gonna sing for his suffer!" Raoul sniggered.

"I insist this paid killer be handed over to me," Antonin's thickly accented voice cut in. "We have old accounts to settle. His life is forfeit ten times over...but that is a matter I intend to deal with personally."

"Very well." It was clear that Jean-Paul was struggling to master the anger that had swept over him at the discovery of "Sondermann's" double deceit. "But first there must be explanations. And quickly. We have more important things to discuss than traitors."

"Don't bet on it," Bolan said evenly. "I'm sure you won't like the explanations."

He had long ago decided on the strategy he would employ if his true identity was discovered. And it had occurred to him that even if the worst arrived, it could still be turned into a plus.

"We are waiting," Jean-Paul said harshly.

Bolan could see his hands clenching and unclenching at his sides, symptoms of that nervous instability Bolan had several times filed away mentally as being potentially useful. He was determined to play on it now.

"I am Mack Bolan," he said.

"The Executioner?"

"Some call me that."

"What the hell are you doing here, passing yourself off as Sondermann?"

"Sondermann was killed in a freeway pileup on his way down here. Like the man said, there's a resemblance. It seemed an idea to take his place."

"Why? Whose idea? What was the point?"

"I was put in," Bolan said truthfully, "to find out what was brewing and why four capos had been killed...and then to mix it so that your big deal with the colonel here fell through."

"What!" Antonin roared. "There! You see! The man is a spy, a renegade, a cheap mercenary. Let me—"

"Easy, Colonel," J-P interrupted. "Your turn later. Let me handle this my way first, okay?"

As the KGB man lapsed into angry mutterings, Jean-Paul turned back to Bolan and asked, "You said you were 'put in.' That means you're not working on your own, that you are, as Colonel Antonin says, a hired man. Who are you working for?"

As long as he avoided any mention of Telder or Interpol, Bolan could still use the situation to confuse matters and sow even more discord among the mobsters.

Instead of admitting that he was working for a law-enforcement agency, he would land the shit squarely in the fan by implicating another mafioso. The hell with denials and proofs and counterclaims: once the accusation was made, doubts would remain.

Bolan's choice was based on the fact that, on the features of a man taken completely unaware, bewilderment, stupefaction and guilt leave much the same pattern.

That and the electric tension that was almost tangible.

"Who hired me?" he repeated. "Renato Ancarani."

The effect of his words was more dramatic than he had anticipated, the result more spectacular than he had dared hope.

A sudden stunned silence followed by a chorus of angry shouts. Then Jean-Paul's voice, shuddering with fury: "Ancarani! Come in here, you double-crossing twister!"

The Corsican was in fact still outside on the patio, talking to a group of hardmen. He had taken no part in the heated discussions that followed the arrival of Scalese and the man with the bandaged throat. Now he pushed his way through into the room. "Who's calling names?" he cried angrily.

"Silence, you goddamn Corsican traitor!" Jean-Paul's voice was again trembling with wrath. "Your hired man sold you out. What made you think you could get away with it, you sonovabitch—planting a fucking mole on me, putting in this Bolan to wreck our plans from the inside?"

Ancarani's eyes widened at the stream of accusations. His jaw dropped. His hands made ineffectual gestures and although his lips moved convulsively, no words emerged.

Bolan was right. Taken totally by surprise, he looked in his stupefaction to be the picture of guilt.

Jean-Paul drew a Colt Python from under his jacket. "You slimy bastard!" he snapped. And before anyone could stop him he had fired the .357 Magnum revolver twice.

The two 158-grain hollow points drilled into Ancarani's chest before he could get out a word of denial. He choked on blood and fell, his monogrammed silk shirt already a scarlet ruin.

The sharp crack of the shots in the room was echoed by a volley of explosions from Stromboli's distant crater. Once more the flagstones drummed beneath their feet, the porcelain shivered on the chimneypiece. Outside among the lemon trees the short Mediterranean twilight was brightened by pulses of crimson.

Inside the villa there was uproar. Not all the mobsters were for Jean-Paul. Ancarani had his followers, and even the neutrals were yelling their disapproval of the killing.

Young Scalese was shouting loudest of all: the hell with the damned Corsican and what about the raid on his father's house? What about this bastard Bolan and the goddamn baron?

Jean-Paul snatched Bolan's Beretta from Smiler and jammed the muzzle against the big guy's solar plexus. Bolan knew he was once again near death. The mobster's whole body was shaking with rage now.

"I don't get it," he snarled. "You were working for Ancarani? And now I am hearing that is was Etang de Brialy who put you up to it?"

Bolan had once written, "I am marked for death. I am as condemned as any man who ever sat in death row. My chief determination is to stretch that last mile to its highest yield, to fight the war to my last gasp."

Now, when that grim prophecy seemed about to come true, the warrior clung to that resolve: he would inflict the maximum damage possible while there was still breath left in his body; he would wreak as much havoc as he humanly could among the slime-bucket hordes surrounding him.

The hell with those denials: he had laid a hot enough trail for his story to leave at least some suspicions and doubts.

"Yeah," he said calmly. "It was the baron who picked up the tab."

Bolan was used to surprises, but the next move in the game floored him. Jean-Paul turned to the Parisian boss. "Well," he barked, "what do you have to say to that?"

The Executioner couldn't believe his ears. Etang de Brialy said: "Quite correct. I planned the raid and paid this man Bolan to carry it out."

The astounded silence that followed was broken by a high-pitched, wailing scream from Coralie Sanguinetti.

The girl was someplace down the corridor. As all heads turned that way there was a colossal thunderclap from the volcano, and the dark outside was split by a dozen different shades of red.

Bolan didn't wait to ask himself questions. Jean-Paul was half turned away. Sensing a minimal relaxation of the pressure on his biceps, Bolan pinwheeled both arms violently—back and then over, like a discus thrower—hurling Smiler and Raoul forward above his head to crash heavily to the floor on their backs.

While they struggled, half-stunned, to realize what had happened, Bolan grabbed the Beretta by the barrel and wrenched it from Jean-Paul's grasp before he could squeeze the trigger. With a long, looping left that carried all his weight—and all his impatience at the enforced in-activity he had suffered—he dropped the French mafioso.

Then, before Antonin or any of the assembled mob-sters could collect their wits, he shielded his head with both arms and hurled himself through the picture window into the night.

18

The warrior hit the terrace in a combat roll amid a shower of exploding glass, springing up between the two nearest trees to find the whole sky behind the crater above throbbing with orange fire.

The crater lip was a jagged loop of pulsating white heat and from the interior of this hellhole a constant stream of molten rock fountained into the air accompanied by subterranean rumbles as loud and menacing as the detonations of an artillery barrage. Bolan could see a fiery river of lava bubbling slowly downward from some split far up the mountainside.

Racing away, he glanced hastily right and left. This was no time to marvel at the awesome forces that could melt rock to a blazing liquid. Already the mobsters had knocked the last shards of glass from the shattered window and spilled through into the garden after him.

It was quite dark now on the seaward side of the island, a moonless night lit only by the fitful glare from the erupting volcano. Three terraces below the lemon trees shielded the Executioner, a rocky trail girdled the tiny harbor, but there were guards strung along the track, cutting him off from the power launch and the other boats moored there. More men surged out from beneath the arbor as he watched, racing along the lowest terrace to encircle him and block his retreat from the villa.

He could hear Jean-Paul and Zefarelli shouting orders. Dim shapes fanned out at the rear of the buildings, scattering over the higher ground to bar his way to the village.

The only route open to him now was upward—toward the flaming inferno that was boiling from Stromboli's crater and filling the night with the stench of sulfur.

Bolan scrambled up the stone wall retaining the terrace above him, ran across the narrow strip of black earth and climbed again. Torchlight beams lanced the darkness between the lemon trees below.

Above the house on the village side there was a confused hubbub. Once again he heard Jean-Paul shouting commands, and another voice—Smiler's?—repeating Etang de Brialy's name. Suddenly winking points of fire sparkled all around the villa, and a fusillade from rifles and automatics punctuated the roaring explosions from the crater above.

Bolan hurled himself flat...and then realized the shots couldn't possibly be aimed at him. Not yet. They were in the wrong direction and too far away. He rose cautiously and continued, terrace by terrace, his silent upward progress.

Perhaps Ancarani's goons had taken the opportunity to open fire on J-P and his men? If so, that was great...but where was Etang de Brialy?

No way of telling. What was certain was that they—or some of them—were still after Bolan. The flashlight beams were probing the hillside now, sending shadows from fruit trees and vines leaping over the old stone walls.

More shots. A cry of agony. From outside the smashed window a stream of orders ending with the words, "Whatever happens, bring in that bastard Bolan dead or alive."

The soldier was high above the building, threading his way between the wires on a terrace where the vines had long ago run wild, when the lights focused on his position. He ran for the next wall.

It was about six feet high. As he climbed hurriedly, his foot dislodged a stone. Bolan cursed, slipped—and a whole section of the ancient buttress collapsed in a shower of pebbles and dust. In a momentary lull stilling the eruption above, the clatter of falling stone was appallingly loud.

A triumphant shout from below and a volley of shots, this time undoubtedly aimed at him. A near miss ricocheted away with a shrill whine, and several slugs hummed past uncomfortably close.

He was now on a wider strip of land. On the far side, a small, square structure was silhouetted against the flames: a black rectangle blotted from the burning sky.

It was a stone cabin, no more than fifteen feet square, with no windows and an open doorway. Part of the roof was gone now: smoke tinged with scarlet was visible through the gaps.

Bolan crawled in and thumbed off the Beretta's safety.

This time the auto loader was fitted with a 20 round box magazine. But those twenty shots were all that stood between Bolan and death. It depended on how long the mobsters continued firing at one another. But there were, he knew, automatic rifles and at least one SMG backing up the handguns down there. Grenades, too, perhaps.

To fire now would reveal his position. And until the moon rose much later, to remain invisible offered the best chance he had of getting out of there.

But the hunt had already been vectored in the right direction by the collapsed wall. It could only be a matter of time before the flashlight beams swept over, and then into, the cabin.

Bolan's problem now was twofold. He had to figure out some way to get out of there. And fast. Or he could work his way back down in the hope of worsening still more the Mafia position in relation to the KGB.

His brief, after all, was to create discord to the point that the Russians refused to play ball any longer, and he had no means of knowing whether that point had been reached.

He was pondering the alternatives when a familiar voice spoke softly in the darkness behind him.

"It would be best to leave this shack as quickly as possible. Once they know we are here, a single grenade lobbed through that doorway would be more than enough..."

Bolan whirled. "De Brialy! How the hell did you get in here?"

"I was here before you were," the Frenchman said. "A lot of fellows down there would be happy to see me dead."

"Why?" Bolan demanded brusquely. "Why did you agree that you sent me to rough up Scalese? You knew damned well that story was a lie."

"It was on the spur of the moment," Etang de Brialy confessed. "It occurred to me that I could capitalize on your lie."

"What do you mean, capitalize? When it meant you'd be run out of the house with three dozen heavily armed gorillas on your tail?"

"That suited me fine. It was just one more piece of Mafia craziness, all that shooting."

"I don't get it. What's your angle?"

The shooting had stopped now. The flashlight beams were stationary. The volcano crater, still pulsing redly, remained silent.

"We run a clean racket in Paris," the baron replied. "No underage kids in the houses. The shit we push is what we say it is, not cut to hell. The gambling's honest: there's no point rigging it—the house wins, anyway. Guys who pay for protection do get it. No bystanders are involved. There are no muggings in our territory: any free lance who steps out of line is very severely...disciplined.''

"Well, great for you," Bolan said sarcastically. "And so?"

"We work with certain families, but we are not actually Mafia. I think that should be obvious," the Frenchman said with dignity. "My...associates...don't go along with this KGB tie-up. Nor do I. We are, after all, first and fore most a *French* association. We don't want any part of some deal that could mean we're told what to do and when to do it by damned foreigners. No offense to you, sir."

"You mean..." Bolan began.

"I considered that I could work as a...modifying influ ence more successfully from the inside, as it were, than if I made my opposition public, the way Scotto and Balestre and the others did. It would also be somewhat safer." Etang de Brialy's tone was wry and dry. "Of course until tonight I had not actually been able to achieve very much. Simply a word here, a doubt there. But—"

"Are you telling me," Bolan interrupted, "that you're working against the merger?"

"Things are satisfactory as they are. A neat, tidy life with no complications," the baron said primly. "Why spoil it for nothing better than money? We can get that anytime."

"Then, at least for now, we're on the same side. Be cause you must know now that my own—" The Execu tioner stopped in midsentence. Somewhere below voices were raised in argument. Inside the villa a door slammed.

"Impossible, impossible!" Antonin's harsh accents carried clear to the cabin on the night air. "The situation is totally unacceptable."

The next few words were lost because Jean-Paul's furious voice kept interrupting. From time to time contemptuous phrases from the Russian punctuated the gang leader's outcry.

"Acting like children in a slum...absolutely essential that we deal with adults behaving as adults...public killings, bomb attacks, open gang warfare here, in France, in Italy, in California... An intolerable situation."

Bolan lost the thread again as Jean-Paul's near-hysterical argument drowned the KGB officer's words. Then, quite clearly, the mobster yelled, "Your whole aim, you said, was to promote insecurity and chaos!"

"Not among yourselves, you imbecile!" Antonin shouted. "We will deal only with a *unified* organization. Yet here you present me with quarreling, feuding, shooting. Worst of all, you allow the mercenary Bolan to infiltrate your own group."

Jean-Paul's reply was lost in the angry stamp of booted feet on the flagstones. Antonin was striding away from the villa.

Eventually, over the Frenchman's impassioned arguments, his distant voice could be heard icily declaiming, "No! You have shown yourselves, all of you, undisciplined, stupid, unreliable. Now it is over. I shall report to my superiors that on further examination the project has been found to be unworkable."

A fresh outburst from Jean-Paul. Was he pleading, cajoling, even threatening? There was no way of telling: the two men were now too far away for individual phrases to be recognizable. All that Bolan and the baron could say with certainty was that the tirade was cut short with a single sharp expletive in Russian, followed instantly by a shot from a heavy-caliber revolver.

Silence.

Receding footsteps.

A gruff, guttural command, and then the rising whine of a turbojet cutting in.

A minute later the Soviet helicopter rose into the air over the landing stage and flew away toward the southwest.

Before the noise of its rotors faded, the volcano renewed its eruption with a rumbling bellow that shook the ground beneath their feet and sent flames and molten debris shooting upward from the crater.

"Did he kill Jean-Paul?" Etang de Brialy's voice could scarcely be heard over the uproar.

"It sounded that way," Bolan said cheerfully.

In the darkness of the cabin behind them, suddenly a third voice spoke.

"You'd better get out of here fast: they're setting up a searchlight down there, and this is the obvious place to look."

Coralie Sanguinetti!

"How did you get here?" Bolan exclaimed for the second time that night.

"There's an underground passageway. It leads here from a ruined chapel on a rock above the house."

"Could we go that way?" the baron asked.

"Yes. There's a place where the roof of the tunnel has fallen in. About halfway, in the middle of an old olive grove. We'd have some cover if we scrambled out there."

"We?" Bolan asked.

"Yes. I'll show you the way. Your only chance is to make it to the other side of the island—over the shoulder below the crater, and then down to a creek where they keep a couple of fishing boats."

"Below the crater?" Etang de Brialy repeated nervously.

"Some way below. We'll be all right. But hurry...."

Coralie stopped talking. From the roof of the villa below a blinding white beam split the night and began to sweep left and right up the terraces. It was joined by a less powerful spotlight from the bridge of the power launch moored at the landing stage, and then by the hand-held torches that had been searching earlier.

The light from Coralie's own pocket flashlight was shielded by a red silk scarf held over the lens. In the dim illumination Bolan saw in the back of the cabin a trap-door standing open in the floor.

As Coralie lowered herself down the crumbling stone steps, light blazed in through the open doorway. Bolan and the Frenchman followed hastily and closed the trapdoor over their heads.

The tunnel was vaulted brickwork. Despite the proximity of the volcano, the walls were damp, and there were pools of moisture on the floor. It twisted and turned for quite a distance before Coralie's flashlight revealed the slant of rubble and the patch of scarlet sky that marked the place where the roof had collapsed.

They fought their way out into the open air. Red light ahead and white light behind transformed the gnarled trunks of the olives into a grotesque tableau. "The big searchlight below," Bolan asked the girl, "is it mobile?"

"No," she replied. "It's mounted permanently on the roof."

"So once we make the far side of the ridge there's no more danger from the light?"

"No," Coralie said dubiously, "not from the light."

There was plenty of danger on the near side of the ridge. They had made less than fifty yards when the powerful beam brightened among the trees and there was a shout from lower down the slope. They had been seen.

A ragged volley of automatic-rifle fire brought leaves tumbling down from the branches above their heads. "Split up and zigzag," Bolan ordered tersely. "What's on the far side of this grove?"

"Rough ground sloping upward, covered with long grasses, rocky outcrops. There's no more cultivation," Coralie said.

"For how far?"

"In height? Maybe another eight hundred, nine hundred feet. After that, it's volcanic stuff: old lava flows and ash."

"Let's go," Bolan said.

Because it was all over now except for the shouting. He could report that the mission was accomplished; the Soviets abandoned their project and the enemy forces were in disarray.

Those forces who were not actively tracking him down, anyway, with orders to bring him in dead or alive. Maybe, Bolan thought, instead of just getting the hell out, he would stick around awhile first and try shouting a little....

At the far end of the olive grove he dropped to one knee. The power launch was way out of range now, but flashlights were still bobbing around and the big searchlight silhouetted shadowy figures among the trees. Bolan let off a couple of rounds and thought he saw one of the figures stumble and fall. Etang de Brialy, who was carrying a Detonics .45 Combat Master, pumped half a dozen rounds in the same direction.

As their fire was returned, the two fugitives ran out from under the trees and followed Coralie, who was already wading through waist-high grasses.

Out in the open, Bolan realized that the wind had risen. The tower of black smoke billowing from the crater was now leaning over to the northeast, and the incandescent fragments showering thunderously skyward were all falling on the nearer slopes of the cone. From this position high on the mountainside they could look over the basalt headland to the riding lights of *Bloody Mary*, where she lay rocking at anchor in the freshening sea.

The night had been warm; the hot wind blowing down from the active cone was suffocating. By the time they at last breasted the ridge, each of them was soaked with sweat.

The darkness on the far side of the crest was relative. Instead of the harsh searchlight brilliance, the ground was suffused with a wavering red glow reflected from the underside of the vast cloud streaming from the erupting crater.

Immediately below them, a wide, shallow depression separated the ridge from high ground overlooking the sea on the far side of the island. And, as Coralie had warned, it was a lunar landscape, witness to countless eruptions in the past, which had inundated, stratified, seared and tortured the surface until now it resembled nothing so much as a giant black Christmas cake whose frosting had been whipped into frightening shapes by a fork.

At the upper end of the depression, glimmering in the tawny light, a fresh flow of molten lava dripped heavily from crag to crag.

"We take this path," Coralie called over the express-train roar of the volcano. She began edging down a narrow shelf of rock that slanted across the face of the depression.

Following close by, Bolan took in with pleasure her slender form, clothed now in tight-fitting jeans and lightweight T-shirt, her dark hair tied back with a ribbon that matched the shirt. "That scream," he said, "just before I busted out of the villa: it was you, wasn't it?"

"There was nothing wrong," she said. It was the only thing I could think of to make some kind of diversion."

"You probably saved my life," Bolan said. "How come?"

Coralie turned to grin at him. "As soon as I knew you weren't that German hit man, that you were not a killer for hire, I figured my first impression must have been right, after all. When I found out you were doing your damnedest to wreck this Russian deal, I decided to help all I could."

"You were trying to wreck it yourself? All the time?'

"Not exactly. I just wanted my father out of it. When he's away from these creeps, he's nice. But if that KGB merger had gone through, he'd have been in over his head, and I couldn't stand for that."

"You figure he's out of it now?"

She smiled again. "After tonight—and after what happened at La Rocaille—I think he'll be a little more careful next time he has house guests!"

They were two hundred yards along the shelf. Each time the volcano blasted out its flaming debris, bright glares of scarlet and crimson augmented the pulsating ruby light so that the rocky landscape seemed constantly to change its shape.

What didn't change at all was the compact squad of men positioned on a lava platform some way farther on and a hundred feet below. The ruddy light glinted now bright, now faint, on the metalwork of their guns, but the hands holding guns were as steady as the rocks themselves.

"Damn," Coralie said. "That must be Ancarani's buddies. There was a jeep at the villa. I guess they hot-footed around the coast to cut us off."

"Cut us off, or cut off the gorillas chasing us?"

"Both, probably," the girl said. She glanced behind them. The pursuers had already appeared above the rim, were filing down onto the pathway. "We've got to make a trail on the far side of the valley. It looks like we'll have to quit this path and scramble down among the boulders and up the other side."

Bolan heard the shooting when they were only a few yards below the shelf. Muzzle-flashes were invisible in the leaping light, but the reports rebounded from the walls of the canyon like minor echoes of the detonations shaking the crater above.

The pro-Ancarani group on the lower platform numbered eight or nine; there were probably at least a dozen on the way down from the ridge. Smiler and Raoul would be among them for sure, and at one point Bolan caught sight of the great bulk of Delacroix.

"Do you have a gun?" he asked Coralie.

"No."

"Then you better make it to the floor of the depression," he told her. "Stash yourself in among those boulders—" he pointed to a cluster of tall rocks "—while we see what we can do for the opposition."

She nodded and hurried on down amid a scattering of pebbles and stone fragments. Etang de Brialy carried spare clips for his Combat Master. He was already blazing away at the mobsters working their way down from the ridge, firing two-handed with his elbows supported on a pumice outcrop.

Bolan had to be more careful. He knew he had to make every shot count. There were eighteen rounds left in the magazine, and unless he could liberate a gun from the attackers, that was it.

Both groups had seen them leave the pathway; both were unleashing a murderous hail of lead down the valley. But they were also, crazily, firing at each other.

The Executioner smiled grimly and prepared to join in. It was the first time in his life that he had been involved in a battle where he could fire—was obliged to fire—on both sides at the same time; and the second time, after the Corsican adventure, that he didn't give a goddamn which side won!

As long as his own small group survived.

Squinting against the deceptive light, he fired half a dozen rounds at selected targets. Or what he figured were targets. There had already been casualties on both sides, but the changing rock silhouettes, the moving shapes of men, the bounding shadows, swelling and dwindling with the glow from the cone, made it impossible to see how often he scored. He would have to wait until they were at closer quarters before he could be certain.

That wouldn't be long.

Crouching behind rocky projections...running, bent double, from boulder to buttress...the two groups were fast approaching each other—and the fugitives clinging to the valley side.

"You keep after the guys coming down," Bolan called to the baron. "I'll see how many I can take out on the other side." Sighting carefully, he fired twice more at the gunmen on the platform. One at least, he could see this time, spun away from his fellows and collapsed on the basalt shelf.

"I'll do my best," Etang de Brialy replied. "Shooting against the fireworks from that damned crater makes it difficult. But that big bastard Delacroix is the easiest mark. If I could—"

The sentence was unfinished. After a moment Bolan turned around. There was a metallic clatter as the heavy Detonics automatic slid to the ground. The Frenchman was draped over the pumice.

As the Executioner touched him he flopped limply away, a fist-sized hole gaping horribly in the back of his head. Two sightless eyes stared blankly at Bolan; a third, making a neat triangle with the other two, yawned blackly at the top of his forehead, expressionless witness to the high-velocity slug that had blasted his brains away.

Bolan cursed. He laid down the body, took the gun and the spare clips and scrambled farther down the slope. Without the baron to cover his flank, he would be enfiladed if he stayed that near the pathway.

It was curious, he thought as he headed for the rocks where the girl was hiding—the Frenchman had been involved with drugs, prostitution, gambling, protection. He was a classic underworld racketeer. Yet somehow Bolan could not resist a sneaking admiration for him. Even if he hadn't achieved much, he'd had the guts to take on the whole of the southern Mafia.

It wasn't just because he desperately needed a backup that the Executioner would miss him.

Among the rock columns on the floor of the depression the eruption seemed nearer and more dangerous than ever. The hot wind blowing down from the cone dried the inside of Bolan's mouth with sulfurous fumes and choked his nostrils with fine ash. Trapped gases forcing their way through the viscous molten magma inside the crater were now escaping with explosive violence, hurling fountains of liquid fire high into the night sky.

The gunmen on Stromboli had changed their tactics. Although most of the gang descending from the ridge were already below the pathway, they had switched their line of attack to concentrate on the remainder of the Ancarani group. The Sicilian boss, Arturo Zefarelli, was shouting orders. The liquidation of Bolan and the girl would be much easier if the dissident mobsters on the platform were eliminated first.

He found Coralie among the rocky pillars. He asked her, "Can you handle an automatic?" When she nodded, he added, "Take this one. The recoil is rugged, but the Baron's .45 is tougher still."

He handed her the Beretta. "Don't shoot until you're certain of a hit. There are only ten shots left in the magazine."

Higher up the valley, white-hot projectiles of lava, cooling and hardening as they spiraled away from the crater, were clattering back to the ground and rolling toward the pillars. Between this noise and the hissing of escaping gas and steam within the volcano, the gunshots sounded strangely insignificant.

Soon they ceased, and Bolan saw that the battle between the two rival Mafia factions was over. There was no more firing from the platform. Ancarani's supporters had been eliminated.

For the survivors of Zefarelli's squad—there were nine or ten of them—a single objective remained.

The obliteration of Bolan and Coralie.

The Executioner saw them swarming down the sides of the depression now, spread out in a rough semicircle to flank the rock cluster where they were hidden.

Well, the fact that he was outgunned and outnumbered had never deterred Bolan before. He posted the girl behind a barricade of fragments where two of the columns had split and tumbled. "Don't shoot and give away your position until I open fire," he warned her.

Crouching, Bolan himself advanced behind a rampart of tuff—the solidified residue of a liquid lava so aerated with gas bubbles that it had once formed a molten froth. The porous rock left when this cooled was brittle enough for chunks to be broken off by hand.

Bolan separated a fragment the size of a football and waited. Zefarelli's men were advancing cautiously, not knowing where he was hidden, ducking behind outcrops as they came.

He hefted the fragment, drew back his arm and hurled it toward a channel lower down the valley. The tuff landed with an audible thump, broke into pieces, and rattled down the incline.

At once four or five mobsters pounced, firing as they ran. Bolan was left in the position of an enfilade. Steadying the powerful .45 with his left hand, he blazed off the remainder of the magazine and saw at least three men fall.

But now the enemy knew where he was. Snapping in a fresh clip, he dodged away and took up a new position on the far side of the cluster.

No mistake about the gunshots this time: revolver and rifle bullets hummed between the pillars, splatting against basalt, chipping splinters from the rock. From some way off, Bolan heard the girl firing carefully once, twice, three times. Below the pathway a man cursed and then screamed.

The mobsters were closing in. The Executioner knew that unless they were to be trapped, he and Coralie must retreat up the farther valley wall toward the trail she was looking for. But this meant they would have to quit their shelter. Bolan dropped to his hands and knees below a hail of lead and crawled to the rear of the rock cluster to see what cover there was on the far side.

Suddenly he was aware that Coralie was no longer firing. Bolan strained his ears to listen.

It was then that he heard the scream.

Coralie's voice.

Bolan rose upright and ran to the barricade of rocks where she had been positioned.

There was no sign of her.

He looked up the slope toward the crater...and saw Delacroix with the girl, kicking and screaming, slung over his shoulder.

The mobster's head and shoulders were outlined against the pulsing red glare. Bolan lifted the Combat Master slowly. In the shifting light, he was going to risk hitting the woman. But he had to try.

An abrupt flare from the crater as long flames streamed out in the wind made up his mind. In the brighter light he could see more of the big hood's body. The Executioner held his breath, aimed well below the shoulder supporting the girl and squeezed the trigger.

Delacroix cried out, clapping his hands to his left arm and allowing Coralie to drop. She fell on her feet, staggered and then lost balance on the edge of the outcrop and plummeted to a lower level, where she hit her head on a smoothly rounded boulder and lay still.

Delacroix was swaying, reaching for the gun in his waistband. As the glare subsided, Bolan dropped him with a well-placed round.

Zefarelli was calling again. "Close in! Surround those columns! Flush the bastard out!"

Bolan sprinted across the tortured surface of the valley floor toward the unconscious girl, shooting blind as he ran.

He was wearing combat boots with his summer rig. It was the odor of burning rubber that tipped him off, even before he sensed the fiery heat under his feet.

At the same time he became aware of the ground shaking, trembling, and saw small spirals of vapor rising all around him.

He was standing on the surface of a fresh lava flow!

Streaming from a fissure below the crater, the flow had made it this far already. The outer layer, congealing, cooling and partially hardening in the air, had formed a dark crust.

But beneath, Bolan knew, the magma, still glowing at 900 degrees C, the temperature of melted gold, would still be tunneling relentlessly downward.

He leaped for the sheet of basalt where Coralie was lying, beating out the flames that had begun to lick the outside of his boots. On the far side of the rock the ground was visibly in motion, a sinister, sluggish flow the color and consistency of molasses, with occasional patches of cherry red.

She had fallen between two advancing tongues of lava.

Bolan felt her pulse. She groaned feebly and stirred. There was an ugly bruise on her forehead but the skin was not broken. Fortunately the boulder had no sharp edges and she had merely knocked herself out.

He looked hastily around them. For the moment they were shielded by the outcrop on which Delacroix's body lay. But they had to move fast, and as soon as they did it would be open season for hunters.

To cross the flow that still glowed with inner fire was out of the question. The other tongue had supported Bolan on his own and running. But he doubted that the crust would hold up if he moved slowly, with the extra weight of the girl in his arms. That left two alternatives: advance toward the enemy, or make it up the valley wall, where they would be sitting ducks.

Before Bolan could make a decision a violent blow between the shoulders sent him crashing to the ground.

One of the mobsters had jumped him from a higher shelf of rock behind.

The guy would have done better to have risked a shot.

The impact sent the Detonics spinning from the Executioner's grip, but the attacker also lost his hold on the Kalashnikov assault rifle he was toting. That left them even: the element of surprise was in the hood's favor, experience on Bolan's side.

It was no contest. The mobster grabbed for Bolan's windpipe, kneeing him in the lumbar region. But the warrior twisted onto his back, slashing upward with the edge of his hand to break the choking grip. He planted the hot soles of his boots in the guy's belly and flexed his knees.

The attacker was Smiler—his features twisted into a mask of hate, the red light of the volcano reflected in his maniac eyes.

For a timeless moment they stared at each other. Then Bolan kicked with a savage thrust, and Smiler flew over his head beyond the rock, to land on his back in the center of the solidifying flow Bolan had crossed.

Even then the mobster might have gotten away with it...if he had lain still or tried rolling slowly to the side of the flow. But he panicked and sat up, struggling to push himself upright, and put all his weight on one foot.

The foot broke through the crust.

Smiler sank to his knee in red-hot liquid magma.

Before the animal shriek had burst from his lips, a sheet of flame shot up the whole length of his body, consuming his clothes and setting fire to his hair. He thrashed, wildly waving arms already ablaze. And then pitched forward into the seething hellhole he had made in the flow.

Bolan closed his ears to the dreadful sucking gurgle as the lava closed over his jerking body and carried him slowly away.

Still sprawled on the rock, Bolan turned...to see Raoul standing, revolver in hand, on the shelf where Delacroix lay.

"Too bad for Smiler," Bolan shouted, playing for time as he felt desperately around him for the fallen Detonics.

Raoul raised the revolver.

Ten feet away Mack Bolan stared up at the small, round, black hole of death.

"This is where you get yours, smartass," Raoul snarled.

The shot was deafening.

Raoul leaned slowly forward and fell face down, his arms and legs spread, into the hotter of the two tongues of lava. Flaming, he sank without trace, leaving a whiff of roasting meat to spice the odor of sulfur in the overheated air.

Bolan shook his head to chase the ringing from his ears. Immediately behind him, Coralie laughed shakily as she leaned against the boulder with the smoking Combat Master in her hand.

There was no more shooting after that. Like so many crooked bosses, Zefarelli was only brave when he held the upper hand, using the guts of his forward troops instead of his own.

Bolan had seized the Kalashnikov and sprung to his feet, but as soon as he saw he no longer had a numerical advantage, the Sicilian fled. It was only five minutes later that he became visible—with his remaining soldier, supporting a wounded man between them, moving as fast as he could up the far side of the depression, heading for the pathway and home and safety.

Bolan looked at the rifle. It was an early model AK-47. There were three shells in the magazine.

He bit his lip. Retreating troops? From behind? What the hell, in his position the gorillas would have shown no mercy. And wasn't he, after all, committed to the elimination of the Mafia? If none of them were left, they couldn't reopen negotiations with the KGB....

He raised the gun to his shoulder and fired three times.

At last he swung around to face Coralie. "Let's get out of here now," he said.

Two hours later they stood on the edge of a low bluff above the ocean, looking down on a crescent of black volcanic ash on which two small fishing boats were drawn up.

The wind had died. Above and behind them, Stromboli still growled and spat fire. Out across the dark swell of sea, the faintest of lights showed on the horizon.

"Tropea," Coralie told him. "It's about thirty miles. On the bleakest part of the Calabrian coast. You'll be safe landing there: it's so far off the map that the Mafia have never even heard of it!" She glanced at the beach. "The smaller boat, the blue one, has enough gasoline to get you there."

Bolan had an arm around her slender shoulders. "It's a long ride," he said. "I might need company. How does the idea of a long, cool drink in a bar on the Tropea waterfront grab you?"

She smiled, reaching up to touch his face, gazing for an instant at the rakish, hawklike profile. Finally she sighed and shook her head. "Some other time," she said softly. "In Rome. In Paris. In Marseilles. Who knows? Right now I have to make it back to my father: he's going to need all the help and comfort he can get in the next few days."

Bolan nodded. "Okay," he said. "I'll take a rain check."

He ran down to the beach, pushed out the boat, climbed on board and waved once at the small, solitary figure on the bluff. Then he started the motor and settled himself in the stern with the tiller under one arm, setting a course for that distant light on the mainland.

And the next battle.

MORE ADVENTURE NEXT MONTH WITH

MACK BOLAN

#86 Hell's Gate

Race with death

Enemy bullets have left Mack Bolan seriously wounded. Weak from blood loss and with a fever approaching danger point, he has to keep running without medical aid.

Faceless gunners relentlessly pursue the Executioner across the U.S. border into Canada, where Bolan is caught in a deadly trap: stop and be cornered, or die from his injuries.

DON PENDLETON'S EXECUTIONER
MACK BOLAN

Sergeant Mercy in Nam…The Executioner in the Mafia Wars…Colonel John Phoenix in the Terrorist Wars…Now Mack Bolan fights his loneliest war! You've never read writing like this before. By fire and maneuver, Bolan will rack up hell in a world shock-tilted by terror. He wages unsanctioned war—everywhere!

GOLD
EAGLE

MORE GREAT ACTION COMING SOON

ABLE TEAM

#21 Death Strike
DIE, UNOMUNDO!

Carl Lyons is a prisoner of the Fascist International, and his longtime nemesis Miguel de la Unomundo is offering the Able Team vet an escape from his brain-twisting torture.

The pain was the hammer and the anvil between which Unomundo would smash Lyons until his sanity shattered. And then he would remold the antiterrorist specialist in his own image.

If a man sells his loyalty, he'll sell anything... or anyone!

Here's what reviewers are saying about Mack Bolan, the Executioner.

"In the beginning there was The Executioner—a publishing phenomenon. Mack Bolan remains a spiritual godfather to those who have followed."
—*San Jose Mercury News*

"Anyone who stands against the civilized forces of truth and justice will sooner or later have to face the piercing blue eyes and cold Beretta steel of Mack Bolan, the lean, mean nightstalker, civilization's avenging angel."
—*San Francisco Examiner*

"Bolan excels!"
—*San Francisco Chronicle*

"Millions of Americans are turning to the incomparable Mack Bolan. Required reading in Washington policymaking circles!"
—*Baltimore Sun*

"Not much remains of the U.S. Marine camp in Beirut a year after a suicide truck bomber killed 241 Americans as they slept on a sunny Sunday morning, October 23, 1983. Scattered in the rubble are remnants of fatigue uniforms, torn plastic bags from packaged military meals, scraps of government forms. And lying in a nearby pile of debris is a paperback book, "The Executioner," by Don Pendleton...."
—*Associated Press*

Take
4 explosive books
plus a
mystery bonus
FREE